Bernard
And
Pat

Blair James

corsair

CORSAIR

First published in Great Britain in 2021 by Corsair
This paperback edition published in 2022

1 3 5 7 9 10 8 6 4 2

Copyright © 2021, Blair James

The moral right of the author has been asserted.

A CIP catalogue record for this book
is available from the British Library.

ISBN: 978-1-4721-5525-2

Printed and bound in Great Britain by
Clays Ltd, Elcograf S.p.A.

Papers used by Corsair are from well-managed forests
and other responsible sources.

MIX
Paper from
responsible sources
FSC® C104740

WEST NORTHAMPTONSHIRE COUNCIL	
80003772297	
Askews & Holts	
BB	

Blair James is a writer and researcher from the UK. *Bernard and Pat* is her debut novel.

Praise for *Bernard and Pat*

'[A] powerful debut ... James never loses sight of the story, which looks at the confusing and sometimes abusive relationship the narrator Catherine had with her childminders Bernard and Pat'
Sunday Times

'[Catherine's] voice is intriguing ... Memory and the tricks it plays are at the centre of this intense piece of writing'
Daily Mail

'*Bernard and Pat* is terrifyingly immersive and brilliant, it reminded me of Nabokov, *A Girl is a Half-Formed Thing* and Barbara Comyns ... An amazing book'
Camilla Grudova, author of *The Doll's Factory*

'*Bernard And Pat* is an exquisitely crafted, beautiful little book, which asks startlingly brave questions about how the past invades our present and makes us who we are'
Elanor Dymott, author of *Slack-Tide*

'Written in short, titled segments, the childlike narration takes us back to her babysitters, Bernard and Pat, and to life after her father died when she was a small girl, lonely and confused in an adult world ... The adult point that begins to disrupt the child's perspective is exceptionally well drawn as the whole picture is revealed, little by little, with growing suspense. Acutely observed, and psychologically on the button. Superb'
Irish Times

J

NESSUN DORMA!

CHLOE

Chloe was showing everyone her new beeper and I hated her. She was ugly. The beeper was a present from her step dad, that makes sense. Bernard and Pat had children of their own, but not of each other's. They would come to the house and sometimes Chloe would make me let her do my hair. Bernard was her real dad and she was older than me. Bernard would say her name Chloe and I hated her and her stupid name. Why did she get to have a dad and I didn't? She had two. She had a real dad and she even had another dad who bought things for her. She didn't deserve them and I did.

BOLOGNESE

One day Mum said I came home smelling of garlic and it made her and Dad laugh. Bernard and Pat had cooked spaghetti bolognese with lots of garlic because Bernard had a funny heart and garlic is good for your heart Mum said and I ate some. Dad how do you laugh

CHRISTMAS

The Christmas tree was so big, much bigger than ours. Thomas Cooper and I sat beneath the tree and that is the only time I can remember him being at that house. Sometimes I wonder if. There were all different kinds of decorations and some were made out of chocolate. I wanted to eat one but Pat said no. So many different colours and Pat said no. Our tree at home was always decorated in just one colour or two or three matching colours. It was boring. This one was how a real tree should be. I think it was a real tree, too, but ours wasn't. Thomas and I were sitting on the floor because the seats were all gone. This was the only time that it was not just me alone on the floor. Thomas's mum came to pick him up much earlier than my mum. I sat alone again on the floor and I waited for so long. My mum said that her mum wasn't a nice mum. My mum said that she worked all the time to give us the life she never had. It meant a good thing really, that I had to wait. The tree glowed but the room was so dark. Nights got much darker then than they ever do now.

CARPET

The carpet in the living room was white. We had to take our shoes off in the hall. I would sit on the stairs to put them back on when Mum came to pick me up and it was always dark. I often had to sit on the white carpet when there wasn't enough room for everyone. I didn't like the slippery noisy leather sofas anyway. I didn't go to the other side of the room much because there was a big glass table there. I wasn't allowed to go near it or sit at it because it was glass. Bernard and Pat would shout in case I broke it. I remember that once I hit my head on the edge of the table and Pat was very pleased that it was not broken. The glass was big and circle and you could see through it. You could see its metal legs coming out of it from the top. You could see the white carpet. The glass looked thick but also thin. I wanted to go near it but didn't like being near it either. When I was near it I would think about it breaking and it would make me upset. And Pat said watch the table and it would make me upset. And Pat said don't break the table and it would make me upset. I don't like glass tables. My auntie Sandra had a glass coffee table and once I ran around and I fell and I hit my face and nose hard on the glass. And Auntie Sandra said oh my god the table and my nose hurt. I don't know why people buy glass tables when they make everyone so angry and so upset.

JAMES

We were sitting on the cream leather sofa in our school uniforms. Will you two stop it Bernard said, Catherine will you stop arguing Bernard said. I sat with my whole body on the seat of the sofa, staring at James's audaciously ignorant face. He stared at the TV screen, at his programme. Life was so easy for him. No one ever told him no. No one ever said stop it James. My tiny fists clenched and dug deep into the cream leather. I hated that cream leather and I hated him. And whoever chose cream leather sofas and white carpet anyway, when their profession was child minding? And who made this stupid programme. My socked but shoeless feet stuck up in front of me and I realized that I probably couldn't cave in his skull with such insignificant things. Instead, I got down from the sofa and then I picked it up above my head, James and all, and I threw it through the window and into the garden. I followed the sofa and I dragged James by his big head out from underneath it and over to the pond. The fishes cannot see the telly from here I said and I pushed his face into the pond and the fish pulled him in until I couldn't see him any more and the bubbles of air rose to the surface and up and out into the sky above me all shining and pink and blue and green like the ones from a tube. And it was so pretty and I wondered how such a wretched, complacent boy could create such colours. Bernard watched from the living room. I walked over to a patch of mud and I stamped my feet in it and my socks got all dirty but I didn't care. Then I stood on the sofa and I smeared it in all good. Smeared that mud in smush smush. That stupid cream sofa. Now the sofa was dirty too. I walked back to the living room and I smeared that carpet as well, and everything was all good and muddy and not white or cream any more. I pushed some mud into Bernard's face and in his mouth and he cried and went upstairs. Then I sat down in the middle of all the lovely mud and I picked up the remote and I put what I wanted on the telly and I brought the fish in so that they could watch it too. Then James said Catherine give me the remote and Bernard said Catherine what have I told you.

CRISPS

I was wearing a yellow checked school dress, and a matching yellow flower in my hair. My school's colour was blue, but I had the checked school dresses in every colour. Pink and yellow, green, blue, and black and red and orange. I even had different blues. I don't know why I was allowed to wear them. I don't remember anything before it happened but I remember the day. It was a special day. Instead of going for dinner with everyone else, I stayed in the classroom. I was five, in reception. Miss Thompson was a nice young woman, kind and enthusiastic, the way a teacher of very young children should be. I stayed in the classroom with her and I knew I was going somewhere but not where, I don't think she said anything about it, just that I was to be picked up soon. She was so considerate. When I think about it now, I try to imagine what she must have felt. She must have felt heartbroken. This is not something that a five-year-old should have to go through. But I didn't know. I can remember Miss Thompson's face and her short curly hair. My uncle David always loved her I think. Maybe that's why he started picking me up from school properly. I wonder where she is. I stayed behind and we must have been painting before dinner, because I was helping Miss Thompson put the big, colourful, squeezy tubes of paint away. I loved paint. I loved those tubes. The smell and the squeezy and the excitement. Dry paint on fingers hard and so dry. What does that mean? That it is wet, and then it is dry? I like painting my fingers because of the cold wet of the brush cold and soft and wet little cat licking fingertips but softer and wetter and colder. Reality has proven that cats' tongues are actually rough and warm and gross. Nothing ever turns out the way you think it will no one ever does what they say. We talked and I felt like I was a good person. I was helping and I was special. She looked up and she said something like oh it's time for you to go now. She must have been looking for the clock, or maybe she looked outside. It seemed so exciting that I was allowed to stay behind on my own with Miss Thompson and now Pat was here to pick me up in a big special black car. It was black and shiny and bigger than other cars, bigger than ours. A bigger black car than Bernard and Pat's big black car. This car was long. It slurped like a snake across the playground. It drove all the way across the middle, and cars never did that usually. Cars aren't allowed on the playground. Pat got out of the back door. I don't know who was in the front seat. If Pat was in the back it must mean that she was little too. It must mean that the person in the front was even bigger than her and definitely bigger than me. Bigger than James and Bernard and Mum. Bigger than Dad. It wasn't Dad. Miss Thompson sent me across the playground to Pat and Pat told me to get into the car. We had to go. I don't remember the inside of the car but my head makes up now that it can remember. It's funny how that happens. I often wonder if I remember anything at all or whether it is all made up. Is my life all made up? I swear that I felt special. The long black car took me to a party and lots of grown ups were there and my brother was there but I don't remember him. I was at a party and I was meant to be in school and there were lots of people and crisps and things. I ate crisps and ran around. I felt so important. It was my special day, with my special dinnertime and my special car that came all the way into the middle of the playground to take me to a party. I was an idiot. Mum said I made everyone smile. As if they could. How could they? They were selfish and rotten and I was selfish and rotten and I still am and if I could give back the car and the paints and Miss Thompson and the crisps and if I could give it all back I would. All I remember is the smiling and the crisps. And Dave Cot and Alan Greenhalgh. The party and the running around. It makes me sick. What choked me was my mum saying years later that Bernard had done a reading. Everyone thought that it was beautiful. There were hundreds of people there Mum said. And how dare they be there when I wasn't. They didn't know. It must have happened because when I think about him standing there and him talking about my dead dad, my dead dad, such a vile and putrid and hateful sickness seeps through my body. And I am scared that my body might turn inside out I feel so sick. It must have happened and they didn't know. My brother was there. And I spend my whole life regretting something that had nothing to do with me. What would I be like now? I hate them and I hate me.

WAGON WHEEL

Pat bought me a Wagon Wheel once but I didn't like it. Pat said I was a waste of money.

SCISSORS

I pushed the Sellotape down and smoothed it over and over and it was really down. No air. Hair. So smooth. I was sitting and doing something. Maybe cutting out paper shapes and sticking them to other paper. I put my head and my face down and my forehead on the table and looked down and my hair hung in front of my face. It's funny because even kids have hair, though it is different from hair when you are older. I pinched some of it between my fingers and the hairs pushed out like feathers and magic and I wanted to be able to hold it properly and it be in my hand and not on my head. I got the scissors and they were yellow and soft. I put my head over the table and over to the side and I pinched my hair and I cut across it and it cut dry and bit by bit falling onto the table. It looked so thick and dark in my fingers but on the table it was thin and nothing. I put my arms around it so that no one could see and I felt naughty. I cut a square of Sellotape off and I stuck it over the hair and it was trapped to the table and it looked so different from how it did on my head. Why do things always have to change? It must have been the end of nursery for

11

that day, because Bernard came to pick me up. Just before he got there, Mrs Ives came over and she saw what I had done and she said what have you done and it was as if she already knew and she told me off. She said you cannot do that Catherine. She said that is naughty Catherine. Don't do that again. And then Bernard came in and they talked for what seemed like hours and they both came over to the table and I tried to cover up what I had done with my hands. Bernard said lift up your hands but I kept them there so tight that no one could get them off. And Bernard lifted them with ease and he shouted at me too and they both seemed very shocked and angry and I didn't understand why it was so bad. But I cried. Bernard said Catherine you must never do that again. Mrs Ives and Bernard stood over me at the table and Mrs Ives looked concerned and Bernard was so tall and it was horrible. And I cried because I didn't want them to think that I was naughty.

LADIES

What did you do today? Mum said. I did a drawing of you and Dad and James and Uncle David and me and Mrs Ives said it was nice and it was on the wall I said. Oh wow that's good isn't it? She put it up on the wall? Isn't that good? Mum said. Yes. And I made shopping with Lego and Sarah Johnson said my hair was black but it isn't black is it it's brown I said. It's brown. She said that her hair was brown and that my hair was black. Cry. Don't be silly, don't take any notice of Sarah Johnson. It doesn't matter what she says Mum said. Okay. Sniff. Then Bernard picked me up and I played farm and then I looked at the ladies with no clothes on with Bernard. What? Mum said. What do you mean ladies with no clothes on? Mum said. Were they on the telly? Was it a film? Was it a Carry On film? Or was it an advert on telly? What do you mean? Mum said. No Mum they were in the book. What book? Mum said. A book with ladies with no clothes on and me and Bernard sat and looked at it on the sofa. And I laughed. What kind of book? Was it a magazine or a book? Mum said. I don't know Mum. I want to watch telly. Did Bernard say what book it was? Mum said. I don't know Muuuum. Okay love it's okay Mum said. As long as you are okay. You weren't scared were you Catherine? Did the book make you feel scared or was Bernard scary? Mum said. No Mum.

BOUNCY

I sat on the little sturdy donkey and bobbed from side to side and I thought this is nice only I could see the others stood waiting and watching me and laughing and it made me feel bad and I felt stupid. They laughed because big kids think donkeys are stupid. And then we went home. We had gone somewhere that day, I don't know why. It reminded me of going on holiday because we were in the car for so long. It must have been the summer holidays. Bernard had driven us in the black car. It was me and Bernard and James and Chloe and Luke and Scott. Now I think about it, I don't know how we all fitted in that car. Maybe Scott was not there after all. He was the oldest. Maybe no one was there. I had sat in the back next to the door, on the side behind Bernard. I don't know why I wasn't in the middle, because that's where the smallest person sits. It should have been great. But there was a spider on the door and it was disgusting and it was so close to me. It moved around and I kept my eyes on it the whole long time. I leaned away from it as far as I could for the whole car and it lasted so long. I needed the toilet. I always needed the toilet then. My mum later bought that black car from Bernard and Pat and I could never forget the spider. I always sat on the other side and I would never tell James why. It was okay because James seemed to like his side anyway. The car had child locks on the back doors and sometimes Mum would forget to open them from the outside and I would be locked in and I couldn't get out. I longed for the spider to be next to James, next to anyone else. It could have just been next to someone else. It didn't belong in that car but then neither did I. I don't know why they even brought me. Necessity. Oh how life seems so miserable. There were all sorts of rides there, at this place that we got to. I remember the bouncy castle, bigger than the usual ones at fairs and on the field in front of our house. It was the first thing that we came to and I went on it but no one else did. The beginning of the day. And I went on the bouncy castle on my own and Bernard stood watching. I always seemed to have to do things on my own. The kinds of things that are only fun with other people. I don't know where those others were. I have this feeling that they were riding go-carts. Bernard told me I couldn't go on any of the other rides and I cried. Oh boo hoo little Catherine. Bernard said that I was too small and I felt so powerless because it wasn't my fault I was so small, and so smaller than the rest. I didn't ask to be. And I didn't ask for them to be bigger. Bernard and I just watched the others go on the rides all day. But I can't remember that. James never liked rides anyway so it wasn't fair. I don't know what we did. I was sitting on the little donkey and everyone was laughing and nothing ever seems to work out. Even the things that seem nice really are not.

BATH

Sometimes after Bernard picks me up we have bath time. There are no toys in the bath like at home but there is more soap. At home I have letters that go on the wall and I have cups to make potions with. Mum told me not to drink the water but when she goes outside I sometimes do. I can't have letters at Bernard and Pat's because there is no wall and I can't have the cups because it will get the carpet wet and I can't drink it anyway because Bernard doesn't go outside like Mum. The bath is not like our bath in the bathroom. Bernard puts it in the living room and then he gets me ready for the bath and he gets ready too and puts me in it. I have to clean myself at home but Bernard cleans me at Bernard and Pat's. Bernard's hands are big and better for cleaning. He says I need to get nice and clean for Mum and he says you don't want to be dirty for your mum do you and I say no. When I am clean I can go on the sofa.

DADDY

Cry cry. What's wrong Catherine are you okay? Oh pet, come here. Pat pulled me in and cuddled me tight. Are you upset about Dad? Yes I said. Oh I know, pet, it's awful isn't it. I know it's very sad and you miss him but he is up in heaven now and God and all of the angels will be looking after him. Pat held me and my whole body fitted on her and she had me bundled up tight and rocked me back and forward and I cried. Do you understand what has happened Catherine? It isn't your fault and it isn't because of anything you've done that he isn't here. And it is very sad but sometimes people go away and they don't come back. Do you feel upset about Daddy a lot? Yes I said. I want him to come back I said. I know Catherine but he's not going to come back, he is in heaven now. That is where people go when they go away and they are in a magical place where everything is okay. And your dad he was very ill and he was in a lot of pain and he is not in any pain any more and that's good isn't it? Yes I said. But you miss him and that's not nice is it? No I said. Cry cry. Dad will be looking over you though and he will be so proud of you for being such a big brave girl and he wouldn't want you to cry would he? Yes I said. Don't be silly. No he wouldn't would he? He wouldn't want you to be upset and crying would he? No I said. So are you going to try and be a brave girl for Dad? Pat wiped my wet face and held my chin to look at her and I nodded into her hand. What a pile of shit. Who are you and why are you here and why is Dad not here? And how I have learned to say what people want me to say and to nod and to do what people want me to do. Or I have at least learned to know what they want, even if I choose to ignore it. Knowing what people want gives you a lot of power. It's always been a game. But this isn't really power, is it? Why can't I be real?

DRIVING CATHERINE

Bernard's arm went straight across my chest like a big barrier and it stopped me short from flying through the glass. I don't know if I was scared or if it was fine. I think that it was too quick to be either. Loads of things were fine then, though. More than now. I was still sad and I was still lonely but I didn't understand those things and so it didn't really feel that way. It only occurs to me now how alone I was all of the time. We were in the big car. Bernard and Pat were Christians. Their cars had fishes on them and the fishes were gold. I had spent the day with Bernard, maybe another weekday in the summer holidays. I never played with friends or I never went to see other kids. I never remember James being there at all. When he was it wasn't a comfort, it made me sad. Bernard and I had rolled out of the drive in the big car that morning. I wonder if Mum knew. The driveway is so stuck in my head. It was a gravelly floor but not gravel and had a path to the wooden door. There were stones and there were huge palm trees in the garden. Their house seemed so far away but as I grew older I learned that it was only a ten minute drive from our house. It seemed like a different kind of place. The palm trees were not palm trees but they had big fluffy white long things coming from them. Mum asked for some cuttings of those plants once and asked and asked again afterwards but Bernard and Pat never gave her any. I don't know why. Maybe it was never a good time. The path also went across and round the side of the house, to the back garden. Our house didn't do that. You couldn't get to our back garden from the front garden and that wasn't as good. We came out of the driveway in the big car and we drove to a place that was on the same street and it was a church. Churches seemed like fun places and they always had bright colours and things in them but I didn't know what they were for. It was just me and Bernard. He helped me get out of the big car and we went inside the church but it was the part at the side that didn't look like a church. Bernard got out lots of bags and boxes and they all had food in them. I had to help carry the bags and the boxes and all of the food to the car and I felt grown up and I liked being grown up. I was small so Bernard probably carried more than me. We filled up the car with all of these things and then we drove around again and this time it was longer. I was a grown up again and I was sat in the front seat and only grown ups sit there. I've always liked sitting in the front seat. Even though James was older I always sat in the front of Mum's car and James sat in the back. He liked the back better, which worked out well for me. Bernard drove to a further away place where they kept big tall long cars and Bernard had one of them. It smelled funny and it was cold and it was a big tall place. It was dark and wet. We put all of the food in the funny long car that Bernard had and it had cupboards in it like our kitchen at home. It was like a room but it was not a house. I had not seen a room like that before. The food went in the cupboards and then Bernard locked it all up and waved goodbye to a man in the big wet smelly place and we got back in the car. We were driving back to the house again and Bernard stopped the car very quickly and I shot forwards out of my seat. Bernard laughed oh ho ho don't tell Mummy about that and laughed. Nobody wore seat belts in those days.

MCDONALD'S

Before Dad died we went to Grandma's on Thursdays but after Dad died we went to McDonald's instead.

PAT

Pat's face rarely smiled. She had a sharp voice and scowled even when she didn't mean to. I wonder what that is like. She said ey a lot. Now I think about it she was very working class. She got on with things and it didn't occur to her whether to enjoy them or not. A woman who had forgotten what she looked like long before. Pat was very businesslike and not at all mumsy. When I was older, I got a new child minder called Sylvie and she was very motherly and very caring but it was too late by then. Sylvie you could have saved little Catherine with your golden heart. Pat was small, not thin but not fat. Little woman. Short hair, salt and pepper. If I could imagine her to be sitting in a chair it would be a car chair, the one with the driving wheel, the chair as far forward as it could go. Looking straight ahead with dead eyes and around and from side to side and alert but not on me. Or a straight-backed, uncomfortable wooden chair. A chair that no one would sit in for long. Sat awkwardly as if waiting to get up. I don't think I ever saw her sitting down apart from in the car. In Pat's car she had a wooden beaded seat cover. I used to think that it couldn't have been very comfy. Pat's face hung long, mouth rested open as if out of breath or preparing for something. I bet that mouth was dry. Small eyes quite close together with nothing behind them. Northern mouth, thin lipped, square face and a pointed nose. No makeup. Never jeans. What did you wear? You look tired. Now she might smile all the time but she didn't then. Hair like a wire brush, short but wild despite her desperate cleanliness and neatness. Mum said she was like a teacher, and that she had been a teacher, and Mum thought that would be a good thing, that she would look after me properly and teach me things. Pat always said what a clever girl I was. Sometimes you call your teacher Mum by accident, and it's embarrassing. Pat wasn't a nasty woman but she wasn't nice either. She liked Heather more than me and I didn't understand why then. I suppose it makes sense now. She wasn't silly or fun.

Bernard used to make her laugh sometimes. She was forever telling me not to do things. I didn't think I was very naughty. I never called Pat Mum.

TOILET

I never went to the toilet at Bernard and Pat's. Or at least that's how I remember it. Cannot remember toilet. I couldn't describe it if my little mind tried and tried, and it did, and I'm still trying. I do remember that I always needed the toilet. And I would hold it in. I held it in at Bernard and Pat's and I held it in all the time. It was never just a little bit, I always needed the toilet so desperate and I hated it. I hate going to the toilet now because it is boring. And I think that I just hate doing anything that I have to do. I hate not having choice and I hate not being in control. When I was young my auntie Bet used to come for dinner on Sundays. We would sometimes go to hers too. I think later we went to hers more, or maybe it was before. Who cares. I didn't care for her. She wasn't cute or little or polite or loving like aunties should be. She wasn't funny. She was big and flabby and her neck wobbled at me when she spoke and she ate in such a disgusting way and it repulsed me. So much skin. Her voice sounded so drastic. She sounded like she had whooping cough. She smelled just like her house and her house smelled horrible. It was like piss and potpourri and gravy and Fairy Liquid and staleness. It smelled like carpet. The carpet smelled. The carpet that once must have been soft and fluffy was now old and it was as if the years had gathered a coating of grease to its hairs. The carpet hairs were much longer than any other carpet I'd known, similar to a shag pile rug that I now have in my own home. The smell. She cared for my brother and me deeply but we both showed her nothing short of contempt. It is sad really. She is dead now. But she was not then, and one Sunday she was at our house and we were watching a Sunday film on telly like every week after dinner. In those days kids watched adult films, unlike now. Now a large group of adults will gather around the television with one sole child and watch a computer-generated film about weevils and apparently enjoy it. This Sunday we were watching *Clash of the Titans* because that's what was on. Channels were different then. I asked Mum to come with me to the toilet and to promise that she would wait on the landing for me. I made her promise because I knew she would break it. I made her promise because you're not allowed to break a promise. I've since learned that promises don't really mean anything. This time, I was particularly scared of going up the stairs to the toilet not only because of the dark and the alone but because the film we were watching was about Medusa and Medusa scared me. Medusa is a woman with snakes in her hair and when she looks at you you turn into a statue. I wasn't scared of being a statue but I was scared of Medusa. Mum walked me upstairs and made her usual empty promise to stay but all I would hear was the steps down the stairs and the bannister creak and the volume of her voice dissipating with distance. Oh I could see Medusa on the landing, she was on the stairs. Snakes writhing and I didn't know what she would do to me but her presence was so foreboding. It is no wonder that I got into the habit of not washing my hands after I had been to the toilet as a child because I would scramble down the stairs as quickly as my desperate and terrified young legs would take me. Toilet became not only a source of fear but of shame. We were on holiday, Mum and James and Uncle David and Auntie Bet and me. And we were travelling somewhere on a bus. I don't know where we were or where we were going. It is likely that we were travelling between Newquay and Truro in Cornwall, between where we were staying and where my mother's relatives lived. Auntie Lyn and Auntie Sandra, Jon, Laura and Daniel. The bus journey was long, as everything seemed to be. We sat along the back seat that ran across the width of the bus. I needed the toilet. I needed the toilet so badly after a certain amount of time that I cried because I was on the verge of wetting my pathetic little self. My mother told me that we could not get off the bus and that I would have to hold it in but I said Mum I can't I can't. It got so bad that my mother had to rush me to the front of the bus while in transit and plead with the driver that he stop or I would wet myself. The driver pulled over at the side of the road where there was an area of woodland. My mother hurried me off the bus and into a bush and I had to squat down and piss on the floor on the soil and try not to wet my shorts. But I was wet. There was no way to wipe myself. There was nothing to do. Nothing I could do but piss out there in the cold and then be led back to the dreadful bus. The physical relief that I felt was short-lived, and was soon replaced by a true and pure humiliation that I have come to feel so accustomed to. Though I cannot remember that the passengers laughed or shook their heads or took pity on me, I cannot remember, either, a fresher feeling of shame. They all knew. They all knew what I had done and what I had been forced to do. If I hadn't needed the toilet I would have been happier. Didn't they understand this? I did not want any of it. So I sat again at the back of the bus, James and Auntie Bet and Mum and Uncle David all chuckling at the situation I had found myself in. Had been thrown into by a cruel fate that pervaded my life. I sat wet and ashamed and cry. And everyone knew. And I wish they were all dead. And I wish that I hadn't been so desperate for the toilet all of the time. Desperate all the time. In truth I should tell you, I am a desperate woman.

JAMES

James you eat so loudly. How do you learn to eat? Learn to eat loud like that. Maybe not learn not to. Don't learn anything. Ski slope head. Words hurt James more than fists and words are all I have ever had. James older and more liked, more likeable perhaps, more attention. Not from Dad. But Dad went away. I did always feel an upper hand over him though and I suspect he always felt that hand too. I could break his little core. I can still, if I want. My brain and sense and perhaps my cruelty always outgrowing his. My tact, my resolve, my ruthlessness. I was always a threat to him, though the ways changed. Are you still crying now James. Do you still fear death

DINNER

There was a dinner lady that I used to cry on. She was a big fat woman with black hair and she wore glasses and she was very nice and she used to cuddle me very tightly. I cried a lot at school but no one else seemed to. At playtime and at dinnertime and at other playtime I would sit on her big lap and she would sit on a rock and she would cuddle me and I would cry cry wet tears all over her. When I got older I would still cry but the dinner lady left. People call dinner lunch now.

SPICE GIRLS

Mum took me to see the Spice Girls film for my sixth birthday, six months after Dad died. But time meant nothing then. I loved the Spice Girls, and so I suppose I was like all other little girls in some ways. I had the tapes and I had pictures and I even had a Spice Girls duvet. I had never been to the cinema and I was so looking forward to it. We went and I had to sit on a funny block on top of the chair and it didn't feel safe and I just wanted to sit on a normal seat and I felt stupid. Because I was small, again. And then it went dark. Black. And so loud. And I didn't like it at all. It wasn't what I had imagined it would be, wonderful and magic and great. And I cried again. Auntie Bet was there and she fell asleep. I don't know how she could fall asleep when it was so loud. The noises hurt. I think that Bernard and Pat used to come to my birthday parties sometimes, too. I usually had birthday parties at a church hall. Maybe they came because they were religious. I remember I didn't like most of the other children that used to come, but back then, birthdays were for everyone, not just people you liked. One year I asked to have a ghosts and ghouls party. My birthday is in January but it looked like a Halloween party. For most of my childhood I thought it was on the seventh, but actually it's on the eighth.

PICKHERNOSEHONTAS

I didn't ask to be a child but I was one. I did things that children do like picking my little nose. I would put my finger in my nose and pull out the snot onto the top of my lip and then put out my little tongue and lick it up. My lip was like a storage area for the snot and I would lap it down smudge it onto my lip bay and then wipe it down into my mouth. My mouth was so small and I wonder if it has ever grown any bigger. I wonder that if anything had happened what it might have been with a mouth too small to be of any use. The snot was wet sometimes and sometimes it was dry and crusty and that was better but I followed the same routine for both. I felt so ashamed, picking my nose, because I knew that I wasn't meant to but I needed to. The things that you want and the things that you are not supposed to do are often interchangeable. I tried to do it in secret, and as swiftly as I could. I remember one time I was sat on the sofa and James was too. James was watching telly. I wasn't watching, I just sat and my nose was full of snot. I crawled to the other end of the sofa. James always sat in the same place, on the same side, near the

31

door. I wanted to sit there too but it was where James sat. He was an idiot. I never understood why we weren't allowed to just take turns. The world doesn't work that way. It seems some people have it all and some just have nothing. There was a wall at the other end, with a small gap between the sofa and the wall. In the gap, on the floor, was a magazine holder. I remember that there were holiday brochures in it, and the Yellow Pages, but that might have been at our house. I sat at the end and dangled myself over the sofa arm because I knew it would look like I was looking at the magazines, and then I picked. Pick, lap, smudge. My head felt funny from being upside down but it was okay. I rubbed the snot onto my lip. I can't remember whether it was wet or dry. I thought what a good idea. I had been so clever, dangling, pretending to read in the security and the concealment of the gap. It felt like I could do this forever. And then, I turned my little face to the side and there was Bernard's big head and big fat face right next to mine. The safe snot place collapsed around me and I was flung back into the rest of the world again. Like when your ears pop. How long had he been there? How he laughed! And he said what are you doing little pickhernosehontas? He laughed and laughed and he looked at James and James laughed too. And I said I'm just looking at the books. And they both laughed and they both knew. And I felt so betrayed and I cried and I said no I wasn't. No I wasn't. I wasn't. But they knew. And it wasn't fair that they had caught me and that they didn't believe me. I still feel very indignant when people do not believe my lies. They didn't understand how I felt. Bernard's face just laughed and laughed and I hated him. I wanted him to stop and he wouldn't. So, because I had not finished picking my nose, I snuffed out all of the snot and I snuffed so hard that it shot out all over Bernard's laughing face and he flew across the room and onto the glass table and it smashed into millions of tiny table pieces all covered in my snot and stuck to Bernard so that he couldn't move. He was glued down with snot and the table pieces stuck into him every time he tried to get up. I turned around to James who was still laughing and I did another big snuff all over his stupid body and head and my snot glued him to the sofa in a big James-shaped glob and turned his blue school jumper green. His hands were glued flat to the sofa how he always sat with his arms by his side and the remote underneath. And I sat and I laughed and laughed at snotty Bernard and snotty James like they laughed at me. Now James could sit in his seat forever and watch his programme forever in snot. Are you happy now James? You have it all. And I laughed and laughed. And I cried and cried because I could do nothing. People hurt me and I can do nothing. I suppose after a while they all stopped laughing and I stopped crying and things went on much the same as usual. And even now, I have only learned to be better at lying. Things do not change, they only stay the same.

COUSINS

Daniel and Laura didn't have child minders; they had my mum and my dad. They had their own mum and their own dad and they had mine too. They are selfish. How dare they have my dad when I didn't even have him. How could they have him more than me. Instead I had Bernard, and I had Pat. I spent more time with them than I ever did with my dad. Mum and Dad would take Daniel and Laura on holidays and they would take them out for tea and to do things that they liked to do. Dad showed Daniel how to play football. James never liked football as a child, but he does now. I think that is his own personal shame. His way of getting Dad back but he isn't coming back little James, no, little Catherine. Dad showed Laura how to rollerskate and play tennis, that is what she wanted to do. Idiot. They ate ice creams and they stayed in caravans and they even played with little us, baby James mainly, little James. Only later was little Catherine, only for a while. Did Dad love them? Laura and Daniel? I ask Mum but I imagine that she lies to me. She says no because she thinks that it will make me feel better but it doesn't. And it doesn't because unless an answer matches my own assumptions and conclusions and delusions then I disregard it entirely. I am of course always right, in being always wrong. I find this very off-putting so I can only imagine what a delight I am to others.

HOME TIME

I waited and waited and waited for my mum and on many occasions Pat had to call to see where she was and I would sit in the dark hall all evening but now I just push her away. It's funny how things turn out. It's hard to explain, how it feels not having a dad and not altogether having a mum. For a long time, I thought that she would die too, because I thought that must be what happens. I thought Dad had died and that then Mum was going to die. But a lot of the time I just wanted to be like the other kids whose mums came to pick them up from school. Who were these people picking me up from school? And why did everyone else have their mum come to pick them up but not us? And why did I cry so much and so often and so all the time? Every now and then, instead of Pat and instead of Bernard, it was my uncle David who would pick me up from nursery. Uncle David is like the family dog that ought to be put down but you continue to feed it and clean up its shit and piss and pay its expensive vet bills and listen to it bark all night. He is now fifty years old but has the brain of an infant. That statement feels almost offensive to the wonder of the infant brain. I think Mum used to give him money to pick me up in a taxi, although the nursery was only a short walk from our house. One day, it must have been one of these days, I waited with all of the others to be picked up and after a while I was the only one left. And I was upset and I cried and the nursery teachers fussed over me. They let me take two toys home that day instead of one because of how upset I'd been. Toys meant little bags with wooden toys or puzzles or games in them. I didn't play with them, they just sat on top of the crisp cupboard until they had to go back. I have become used to things as substitutes for people. I waited for what seemed like hours and hours on end and finally it was David who arrived to pick me up. It was never Dad. I never remember waiting and it being Dad at the end. But it must have been. And now I don't cry cry any more but I worry so much that my mum will die that I push her away in hope that it might not hurt as much and in hope that it might not kill me when the time comes.

SWIMMING

I never used to be able to splash water in my face in the morning, I had to use a flannel. I couldn't swim for a long time. Dad
didn't teach me to swim. I could never ride a bike either. These
are things that dads teach you. My nice Sylvie took me swimming
later, but it wasn't the same. Couldn't put my face in water. Now
I splash water in my face to wake up in the morning but when I
do my throat closes up as if I'm choking.

GET DOWN

You. The living room used to be different but I don't remember it then. The carpet was dark. Maybe they were cleansing themselves. The carpet was dark and the sofa was different but everything was in the same place. I still came into the room and I still sat on sofa and on floor. My head mixes my older memories with the newer carpet and the sofas. Mum said that Bernard and Pat ran a charity and maybe it made a lot of money because the whole living room changed. I want to see the room but I can't. The windowsills are low but still seem high to me. I can see the pond outside. The garden smelled funny but maybe it just smelled like outside.

Outside smells different when you are young. The house smelled like Bernard and Pat. Houses always smell like the people who live there. The stairs went up and then to the side and then up again. When I was putting my shoes on or taking my shoes off I would sit on the stairs and I would try to sit as high up as I could but if I went too high Pat or Bernard would shout at me. Get down. I'd try to creep up step by step, but a step too far always meant get down. The sofas used to be red like blood and a soft feeling like the same as some curtains at a big place I went to once where a man kept shouting that there was someone behind me and everyone laughed but I didn't find it funny. Apart from the sofa had been sat in too many times and it wasn't as soft as it was at first and one time I spilled a drink on it and it went not nice. I wasn't allowed drinks near the sofa or at all. I don't remember ever eating there. At Sylvie's I had Vimto and I had smoky bacon crisp sandwiches or sometimes American chicken sandwiches. The sofa was squashed but it was better than the new big slippery one. The new one wiped clean. The carpet was brown and then it was white.

THOMAS COOPER

Thomas Cooper was a boy. He went to Bernard and Pat's too but not as long as me. I see him as he was when he was about eight but he was about two or three. His mum was nice. Thomas had a mum and a dad. I went to his house once with another boy called Joshua and we played with plastic food, which I liked. You could make sandwiches because there was Velcro on the pieces of food. Plastic ham and plastic cheese and plastic lettuce and plastic bread. I liked Thomas Cooper's house. That day I kissed Joshua on the cheek and he pushed me on the floor and cried and then I cried too. I liked Joshua but he didn't like me and I felt like no one would ever like me again. I would never allow anyone to like me again. Thomas's mum took me to her bedroom and I felt special because I was never allowed upstairs anywhere else. Thomas's mum was nice. She showed me her nice table with her nice things on it like necklaces and bottles and things and she showed me how to put combs and clips in my hair because I was a girl. She let me take one of the combs home and it made me feel so happy. Thomas's mum must not have worked in an office like my mum because she always picked Thomas up a long time before my mum picked me up. I remember hoping and hoping that my mum might get there first one day, but she never did. It felt like a competition. Who is more loved? It was okay at Bernard and Pat's when Thomas was there but he was never there for long and he was shy. He stopped going when we were still very young. I often wonder why. Thomas's dad looked like a man and I liked him. I thought he was Danny from *Grease*. He was nice to me and he used to smile at me and it made me happy and embarrassed. I have always become easily attached to men. One time Thomas had a birthday party on a funny bus outside of his house and there was party food but I didn't like any of it because I had never had it at home. That food, food I would come to know so well, was new to me then. Little fat greasy sausages with sharp sticks poking through them, yellow squares and shiny white circles with sticks too. It was all so slimy and smelly. And pineapple. Pineapple was okay. I knew what pineapple was because Mum liked it. There were sandwiches but even the ones that I liked, like the pink ham ones and the white chicken ones, they tasted different. They all tasted different from how they did at home and they all smelled and they tasted like they smelled. There was the tuna mush which smelled the worst of all. It was disgusting. Tuna smelled the worst. I always thought that kids who had tuna on their sandwiches for school must be poor. There were crisps but instead of being one kind of crisps they were all different kinds all in one bowl. And there was no way of knowing which kind of crisp was which and so I picked one up and put it in my mouth and it tasted like a foot and I spat it back out into my hand. I don't know what else I ate. Mum enthusiastically encouraged me not to like any food that wasn't food at home. I liked the bus though. I never did anything like that for my birthday. There were lots of other kids and there was music. I remember Thomas's mum and dad were there too. When Thomas and I were older we weren't best friends like we might have been. Thomas was very shy. Maybe he didn't like me. I think he thought that I was funny but maybe he didn't. I have never been able to reconcile others' thoughts and feelings. I've never talked to him about Bernard and Pat's. Maybe that is why he didn't like me. We acted like near strangers, a sense of understanding murking the space between us. Maybe I felt that murk alone. One time in school when we were about seven or eight, we were in the classroom. We were in the same class for all of school. And one day we were in a lesson and Thomas wet himself and started crying. We didn't know what had happened, he just started crying and Miss Mitchell took him outside. Then there was all wet on his seat and everyone laughed. And it was so awful. Everyone laughed and all I could think about was how awful it was. And his face was so red and so angry and so crying and so ashamed. And I felt so humiliated for him. And how awful everything is that things like that happen and nobody tells you that there will be days like these. And if I could hug Thomas in that moment and tell him everything is okay then I would. And if I could have stopped that from happening then I would have. Life has continued to be inexplicably cruel. I think about how Thomas must have felt in that one moment in his wet seat with his wet face and the anger and the sadness and the confusion and the paralysing lostness and the forsakenness and I have felt that way my whole life.

SUNNY

It was sunny. I don't remember many sunny days there. I think about the number of days and the weeks and the years and so many hours spent there. I spent so long waiting for Mum. I waited for Dad, too, but he will never come. Another sunny day, a sports day, like many other sports days, I was the only child whose parents did not come. Only, I thought Mum was coming that time. I was so excited. I waited and I watched out for her. I think maybe it slipped her mind or she couldn't get out of work. I cried. Mum said sorry but I didn't want her to be sorry, I just wanted her to be like the other mums who came to sports days. This sunny day was at Bernard and Pat's. And I was so excited again. Bernard said that we were going to the park. This was a rare treat. We were all excited – James, Chloe, Scott and Luke. And me. I ran to the stairs to put my shoes on, but I had been mistaken. Bernard told me that I wasn't allowed to go to the park because I was too small. I said please can I come and Bernard said no Catherine you're too small, the park is for big kids. I didn't understand. I watched as the others got ready to go and

I didn't understand why I was not allowed. I was never allowed to do anything. I was always too small. And so, should I have been big? I cried and was left alone with Pat. She told me that I was allowed to go in the garden instead. But there was no one to play with. I went to go outside and Pat shouted at me to put my shoes on, so I did. I went into the garden, but there wasn't much to do. Pat wouldn't come outside; she just stood at the door. The door was wooden. I ran outside but there was no actual urgency. There was no one to run to. In any case, Pat told me not to run. There was a pond in that garden and most of the time it was covered by a large net. I wanted to go and look at the fish and the frogspawn in the pond but every time I got close to it Pat would say get away from the pond Catherine. She would shout Catherine, away from the pond. I kept running around and over to the pond and Pat would say Catherine don't run be careful. I didn't understand why we could never have things like a pond and fish and frogspawn at home. After a while, Pat shouted at me to come inside. I ran towards the door to come in but as I got closer to it I tripped and I fell and I cut my knee on the sharp floor and I cried. And like an idiot. Like an idiot I ran and Pat told me not to but I ran anyway and so it was my stupid fault. Pat said you silly girl and I cried and she hugged me and rubbed my knee. This must be why I wasn't allowed to go to the park. And as a child I never understood why people would rub you where you had hurt yourself. It only made it hurt more.

LAURA

Laura you miserable, selfish piece of shit. With your smelly feet and your stinking attitude who do you think you are? Who have you always thought that you have been? Was it not good enough for you to have everything? But you didn't and you don't. Do you try to assert yourself, try to sabotage others because you have no sense of who you are, nothing to relate to? Do you feel unwanted? When I was eight you asked to borrow my favourite book. You were a school teacher – oh but not any more poor unwell Laura. You are a failure. Back then, you were a teacher, you taught small children, perhaps about the ages of five or six. Those poor helpless things. Your shoes and your smelly feet. You asked me for my book so that you could read it to your class. My most treasured book. *Can't You Sleep, Little Bear?* It had lived in a box between my brother's bed and mine. The book box. Each night James and I would pick a book from the book box and we would read before we went to sleep. Mum had us signed up to the library by the time we could walk. She says this quite often with pride. I loved the library, loved the shelves and shelves of books, loved the tickets that came inside them, the stamps that the library lady would give to them before we could take them home. But this book was mine, can't you sleep little bear. Can't you sleep little bear? I sent it off to you, in that other place where you live, and I felt so proud to have helped you and to be part of the teaching of your class. But it wasn't good enough for you was it? Where is my book now Laura? I would ask my mum intermittently for years about it. What do you think has happened Mum? Do you think that I will ever get it back? You selfish heartless inconsiderate pointless nothing. I never saw my book again. And the book box wasn't quite the same without it. I had outgrown the childish tale, this is true; but it was mine, my book, my story, my special book, it belonged to me. It was a book about me and Dad. Big bear and little bear. And no I cannot sleep. I shared with you my most cherished and magical possession and you never even explained yourself. You will die alone Laura. Now, you are fat. You are still selfish, but woe is you, you cannot lord it over people as you used to. You ill loser. I remember when you met my first real boyfriend, when I was seventeen, and you commented on how good looking he was, as if it might matter what you thought. As if he might be too good looking for me and as if you might have more chance with him. Who cares what you think Laura? Does anyone care now? Your poor daughter. I cannot help but dislike the child because she is a product of your selfish and ugly being but the poor thing never had a chance. You have such strict expectations of her and show such disdain at any perceived mistakes she may, in her childish way, make. It saddens me to think of the shredded self-esteem that she may have managed to cling onto by the time that she is an adult woman. How dare you do that to her? How dare you be so hard on her just because you have nothing to show for your own life. What do you have to show? You have this poor child, and you have your partner. That poor, poor man. He has loved you for years and years and he has put up with your shit so constantly. He is so constant. But I suppose you are too. You are constant in your inadequacy and your self-regard, your nothingness. You never did leave that boring place did you? You are fat and depressed and crippled and I am a success. You could never be me.

WISE

The eyes that look at you and expect you to do well and though they say that they don't mind if you don't do well, really they must and it doesn't matter anyway. I was untouched by the pain of life then. And I don't know that I felt so nervous. I don't remember my mum being there, but then again I never do. I remember Bernard being there. I think he may have filmed it. That is what I remember. He had a big camera and all of the parents sat on big steps going up the wall. I've never remembered this room in any other scenario. All of the other parents sat and they watched their children. But Bernard stood and he watched me and I was not his child. I was glad that Bernard was not my dad. His voice was scary and he was strange and he used to joke a lot but the jokes always made me sad, or they made me embarrassed or they made me annoyed. They were at my expense. Bernard filmed me on his big camera but I don't think I ever saw the film that he made. I wonder if he still has it. I wonder if we ever watched it together. I wonder if he watched it alone. I can see myself dressed in this little gold gown and my hat, and I can see some of the other kids, and I can still see those big steps. I can see Thomas Cooper's mum and dad but I don't remember what Thomas was. Maybe he was the sheep. I was a wise man and I brought gold and I wore a gold outfit and a gold hat and a big gold necklace. Mum said I looked lovely. But how would she know? I think that gold is probably the most boring out of the three – gold, frankincense and myrrh. And now I think that even then everyone must have been laughing at me, must have thought that I was stupid. Must have known. But then, I was okay then. I used to believe. I used to know what I wanted and I used to do it. And Mum said that you could just leave me on my own and I would just get on with doing whatever it was I wanted to do. She said that when I was a baby I would just sit in my cot and sing myself to sleep. James was the first baby so he needed more attention. I never had to be entertained and I never needed to be shown what to do. Never needed anyone. But I did. I never used to second-guess myself. But I do. And maybe I think so much about being a child because it's not fair that I had to grow up into this. And it's not fair that I have never grown up at all.

SHE LOOKED LIKE A BUBBLE IN A GUM

I used to sing on the toilet but I didn't know words to songs I would sing lettered sounds to the tune instead and I thought it sounded right and Bernard would laugh at me. Dad liked music at home. He made me a mix tape with songs on it once but I thought the words were
sheee looked like a bubble in a gum.

MAD NANA

My mum had a mum when I was little and I used to call her Mad Nana. Her hair was funny, big fuzzy hair, and I would touch it and laugh. Mum said I made Mad Nana laugh too. When I was older I asked Mum about Nana and she told me that she wasn't very nice but that it wasn't her fault. Nana got sad after Mum's dad died and she used to go out to the pub and not come home and when she did it was worse. Mum said that after school one day she found a kitten and brought it home but that Nana had been to the pub and she got angry and threw the little cat onto the fire and it made Mum sad. Nana would sometimes take out the light bulbs in their house so that it was all dark and she would say to my mum and Auntie Lyn and Auntie Sandra that it was because someone was coming to kill them and so they had to be very quiet and sit in the dark and wait. She didn't sound like a very nice mum. I don't remember her very much but I remember her mad hair and her mad laugh and she looked mad. She didn't be mean to me I don't think.

THOUGHTS UPON YOUR FACE

Salty all over my wet face. My face could have been so nice but I am quite sure that time has ruined it. You wouldn't recognize me. I didn't understand why I had to feel so much all the time and why it hurt all the time and why things ever happened. And why everyone laughed. I understood everything but I never understood anything at all. And it felt like maybe everything was different for everyone else. Or maybe it was different for me.

WASHING

Pat would sometimes ask me to help her with things. I was there so often. She still had to get things done. Still had things to do. The washing won't do itself willit. Sometimes I would help her do the washing. The bedding was so big – too big for her even. I would help her fold it up like a game. Hold it out and run together. And hold it out and run together. Maybe Pat didn't run. It was funny being in the house with Pat. Always quiet everywhere. I wanted Pat's attention too but she didn't like playing or doing things or listening to me say things. It was always sunny or sometimes it rained. The bedding has no smell. No washing smell. There was never anything else to fold up. Everything finished so quick. Telly or pens again. Sit in room on my own. Downstairs but sometimes up. Pat was never in the same room as me. I think the other washing was for grown ups. The other washing wasn't a game like the big bedding game.

MUM SAID

Mum said that I liked to do grown up things when I was little. And just because I was little doesn't mean I wasn't grown up. I think that I believed that being a grown up meant that everything would be okay. When you're grown up you have a job and a family and a house and everything is okay. When my dad died I think I thought that I had to be a grown up for it to be okay. Or that when I grew up he would stop being dead. Mum said that James went to football on Wednesdays after Dad died. James only started playing football because Dad had wanted him to but now Dad was dead. You are too late James. Mum used to say that I could have a treat while he was there but all I ever wanted to do was go out for meals. Mum said I used to ask if we could sit and chat like grown ups. But when she asked about what, I would say I don't know. Pitiful. Once we went to a fancy place somewhere that took a long time to get to in the car and me and Mum sat at a table just for us. I had decided that I wanted ribs and they only had adult ones but Mum let me have them anyway. When they came they were massive and Mum said it looked ridiculous to have ordered so much food for such a small child but that I loved them. I couldn't finish it all and got the sauce all over my face. Start so many things I cannot finish and it shows on my face. Mum said I liked us being on our own. I don't know what it means to be a grown up. I still think that everything should just be okay. But it isn't. I only liked playing games where

I was a grown up. House, and shop, and even office. I had a full supermarket with a till and all kinds of food and a fruit counter and I would force Mum to buy groceries and order food from the cafe that was also part of the supermarket. I never wanted it to stop but Mum would sometimes say that is enough now. I liked going to the real supermarket with Mum and going to the real cafe. We went to Safeway and they had a play area but it was dirty and full of kids. I didn't like playing games. Kid games. I was serious. I didn't like playing with anyone else. Other people just got it wrong. I had a tiny ironing board that I would set up in the living room with a little stool in front of it and I would put books and paper and pens and things on it and pretend I was working in an office like Mum did. I also did library. Mum would have to eat a whole box of After Eights so that I could have it to use as my ticket drawer, with hand-made library cards to go in each little chocolate packet. Mum would borrow her own books from me. At Bernard and Pat's I wouldn't do anything. I just sat and thought and made things up in my head. Sometimes I would write or draw. I remember once when it was just me and Pat, I was even allowed to sit at the glass table to draw. Like a grown up. I was more a grown up then than I am now. I can see James's face and he had such a placid face. A child's face. My face always looked as though it was about to ask a question.

CHARITY

You give things to other people but you never gave anything to me

HEATHER

There was a small lump in the back that I sat on and I held on for dear life. It was dark and I would whisper things to Heather. She was younger than me, a doll. I thought of all younger children as dolls. I don't mean that I confused them for things that were not living but I treated them like toys. Dolls to play with and to make do what I wanted. Heather thought it was a game but she soon got upset when she wouldn't do what I wanted. We would both be upset. But I knew how to hurt her. I'm not sure where we were going or who was beyond the dark, but there were two of these lumps on either side and Heather sat on one and I sat on the other. Though you couldn't really sit on them. We had to perch, and then to find other lumps and holes in the walls to hold on to. Everything was metal. Every now and then one of us would fly across to the other side. I remember Heather saying woooah. She would laugh recklessly and with no control as if she had no consideration even for breathing. Sometimes I liked playing with her because she looked up to me, I was grown up. There was no one else anyway. I had to do what everyone else said, but she, she had to do what I said. But what was the use when she wouldn't do what I wanted her to do? How dare she? I would tell her that she had to. She would say she didn't want to. Kahffrin she would say. Kahfriiiihn. I would tell her that she was a naughty little girl and that if she didn't do what I wanted something horrible would happen to her. That monsters would come and get her. When I was older, Heather was replaced by two other little girls. Molly. And another little girl called Heather. I would do this with these girls as well, but with an older and sharper tongue. I was cruel. Heather number two was very quiet, she did not serve the role that children should in entertaining you. She never wanted to play, or talk, or do anything. Molly was a naughty little lovely girl. She would hit and bite Heather number two. They were both about three. Molly would make Heather cry. But I would make them both cry. Tea and Toast and little Heather didn't want to play of course. I whispered some venom to her. There were mothers everywhere but I made sure not to be heard and no one could tell. Heather cried and she ended up crawling into a strange cupboard in the wall of the church hall and wouldn't come out. This annoyed me even more. I acted concerned and she looked at me with a sadness and a betrayal in her eyes that she had no way of expressing to anyone else. But but but taty but but but it was taty and she would point and we would all laugh of course it wasn't taty. The moving stopped and I felt my body relax and my grip loosen from the lumps. I remember the doors opening and the light flooding in and blinding and Pat must have been driving because she told us come on you two. And you would never have known it was day outside. People did a lot of things then that you wouldn't do nowadays. And I wonder if Heather thinks about me now. I wonder if the monsters ever came for her.

YOU CHATTED WITH MY MUM

You and Mum would occasionally touch my head or my shoulder and I can still feel it now, real as though it was happening, real as though I was still three feet tall. Am I not? What is the point in being taller? Growing old? I still feel like that pathetic, helpless, useless little thing looking up around the legs of Mum and you, Pat. You would stand with me in front of those legs, each of your hands on each of my shoulders. You would talk to my mum about things that had happened I suppose. I don't think the things were about me. Maybe Mum spoke about work. I imagine she spoke often of Dad, too. It is hard for a woman to be alone. Hard for a partner to be ripped from your arms, even, perhaps, when you no longer embrace. Oh Mum those dark nights may have been even darker for you than for little me. How does the light get in? I can see your face Pat, see your listening face. You were a good listener, your face showed that. You showed care but not precipitously so. Your seriousness, in fact, only ratified your compassion. You seemed an authentic woman. My mother thought of you as reliable, trustworthy. Were you? It was in these moments, these moments before I left for the day, that I felt you were your warmest. Those hands on my shoulders made me feel safe. Made me feel included in conversation that I was not part of. You and my mother, both stern in separate ways, would agree on various things: on people's impudence, on the shocking nature of unjust actions. I often feel that I am most put out by injustice when it matches something equally unsettling in my own being. Do your teeth chatter when it is cold? I'm sure I remember that they did. I'm sure I remember your face with tears running down its cheeks. But I don't know why. Sometimes I would sit on the stairs and wait for you and Mum to finish talking, and sometimes you would talk for a long time. Oh Mum did you have anyone else to talk to? Oh Pat did you choke on your tea after we left each evening? Every single evening. Not weekends. But every evening. God didn't you get sick of each other? Mum, hadn't I waited long enough?

SPINNING

Don't grown ups understand that it hurts when you're lifted up underneath your armpits? I remember what the floor felt like in the living room. Sometimes Bernard or Pat would tell me to get off the floor but sometimes I had to sit there because there were no seats left. I think that people say different things all the time. The carpet was soft but also hard. Hard like new. Sometimes I would sit upside down on the sofa, with head on seat and legs going up the back. I would push myself so that my head would hang upside down off the edge of the sofa and that was fun. My head felt all funny. My hair would go upside down but never fell off. I liked to drape it against the carpet backwards and forwards, side to side. Bernard would let me do it for a while and then tell me to sit properly and Pat would always tell me to stop it straight away. But Pat wasn't always home. Sometimes I would do it and I would slide slowly all the way off the sofa onto the carpet. Telly wasn't so bad upside down. I did things like that more as a protest against watching James's programmes than because I actually enjoyed doing it, I think. I would do things that wouldn't affect anyone but myself to show my disagreement with something. Socks socks socks. Oh I remember that feeling of socks on carpet though my feet were much smaller then. Carpet has never felt the same since. The carpet always felt new but maybe that is because we were never allowed to keep our shoes on. I can't remember if Bernard ever took his shoes off. Blurry Bernard picks me up underneath my arms and spins me round and it hurts and I say nooo. Blurry Bernard picks me up by my ankles from my special way of sitting and hangs me upside down and I say nooo.

RYAN THORLEY

All the girls loved Ryan Thorley, but in retrospect I cannot understand why. He was a little round bald boy. I don't suppose that he enjoys the same success with women now that he is a big round bald man. We used to play a game called kissy cats in the playground. I wonder if the teachers knew. The boys would usually be 'it', and so they would chase the girls around trying to kiss them on the cheek. If you got kissed you were 'out'. I only ever wanted to be kissed by Ryan. I loved him. I used to write out his name as young girls do. I imagined that he harboured a secret love for me and was only too shy to confess it. I think this way about most men now. Once I went on holiday and bought him some rock in the shape of a full English. I was too scared to give it to him but my mum said that I had to since we had bought it. So, I took it in and presented it to him nervously. I don't think he knew what to say. Of course, he was not privy to my secret obsession with him. He kind of laughed and said thank you and the other boys made fun of him. One time at the end of play when we lined up to go back into class, Ryan came up to me to apologize for something and he kissed me on the cheek. I don't know what he had done but I was upset, and feeling that kiss on my face was a moment of perfection. I think that perhaps this was my first kiss. I was about six. Ryan Thorley was never my boyfriend. He went out with an irritating goody two shoes with a stupid name, a name that you might give to a horse or a dog. And it shredded my heart in two. Who needs a heart when it can be shredded in two? The horse is married now.

DOWNSTAIRS

I was in the car and I think I had just finished nursery for the day. Bernard was driving. We were in the black car. Bernard drove the wrong way back and we went down a funny winding street that I had not seen before. We stopped at a little shop and I cannot remember whether or not I went in but I ended up with a packet of Tangy Toms. I don't think I would have chosen them. Maybe I stayed in the car and Bernard chose them for me. But I can see inside of that little shop. Can see the rows of crisps. I was about four I think, though I don't remember Dad. We carried on in the car round the winding road and it led back to the house like magic. Mum never went this way. The stairs were dark, though it was sunny outside, and I took off my shoes. Maybe Bernard took them off for me. I remember playing with some Lego in the hallway.

Bernard was in the living room and shouted to me, Catherine he called. He called my name.

In my head I can see this as a film. Imagine my tiny body walking from the hallway to the living room and my young face turning to Bernard. Bernard was sitting on the sofa and he said look at this.

He sat slouched in the sofa and his legs were far apart and he wore jogging bottoms and they were grey and they it lay over the waistband of the jogging bottoms. I didn't know what it was and he moved it around a bit. he was calm and quiet and his voice was nice and not scary and he said look at this look at this he said

maybe he said touch it or maybe he asked me do you want to touch it and maybe I said no or maybe I shook my tiny head or maybe I touched it. I think he said go on I can't remember

I remember not wanting to but I wasn't scared. I felt uncomfortable in the way I feel uncomfortable now. As if there was nothing I could do. I didn't know what was happening and I don't know what happened and how could I. I don't think Pat was home

SYLVIE

Oh, Sylvie. When she was a young woman, she worked in a button factory. I always liked the word button and I thought that the job seemed like a nice one for her to have. She was a simple woman but deeply kind, and of unassuming spirit. She had taken up child minding so that she could be at home while her boys grew up. Paul was the same age as me, I think that perhaps I was a few months his senior, and Mark was a couple of years older than us both. I had a huge crush on Mark, of course. His bedroom walls were covered every inch by posters, and he listened to metal music, dressing to match. I think that he liked me, too. I remember he got a job working at an ice cream stand and one day I went to hang out with him there. I would try my hardest to impress him by listening to the right music and wearing the right clothes, but I can imagine that it came across as desperate rather than natural. It looked as though we might date for a while once I got a bit older, but it never quite happened. He's engaged now. I can't remember if we kissed or whether I just thought a lot about kissing him. I often struggle with this kind of discrepancy.

Paul and I were good friends and got on well. We shared a dark humour and became quite close during the years that I shared his mother. Occasionally, we would have dramatic arguments and stop speaking for a few days. Once, we had a physical fight on the field in front of my house. He had said something that upset me and I demanded that he take it back. He did not and so I tackled him to the ground where we rolled around scrapping for a while, until one of my fingernails got bent back in the struggle. I cried and went home. He also cried, and he also went home. Sylvie came round later that day to apologize to my mum. She was a good woman.

So, I spent every day after school at Sylvie's house for another few years. I liked Sylvie so much that I would often tell my mum that I was too ill for school so that I could go and spend the whole day with her. My mum never believed me, and Sylvie knew that I wasn't ill, but there was little either of them could do when I refused to go in. I'd sit and watch TV and eat soup. There was never anything on in the day but I didn't care. Some days little Molly and little Heather were there. I'd help Sylvie take them to Tea and Toast, or amuse myself with them at the house. They mainly annoyed me because they were disobedient.

There was a group of other children that came to the house after school during the time that I was there. There was little Jake, who was several years younger, and who shared a kind of sibling relationship with me. I was his big sister who he at times hated and at times loved, and he was my stupid little brother, about whom I felt the same. I felt sorry for him sometimes, and very protective, as he would cry in fits of rage or feelings of injustice. He lived around the corner and had a young and attractive mother.

Georgina and Harry Russell were an obnoxious pair. Their parents were pseudo-snobs. They had money from somewhere, but were unmistakably common. Their mum was mad, with mad red hair, which she pulled out from time to time due to anxiety, leaving unsightly patches scattered across her head. She and her husband split up around the same time I stopped going to Sylvie's and I saw Tony Russell about ten years later with a much younger woman. While his ex-wife may have been exciting to go out with in the beginning, it turned out that being married to her for so long was simply tiring. Harry was very young and red-faced. He and Georgina were spoiled rotten and behaved accordingly. Georgina was a couple of years younger than me and we never bonded. I wonder sometimes if she wished that we had.

These younger children found that tormenting Mark was an inexhaustible form of entertainment and would play knock-a-door-run on his bedroom door. He would scream and shout at them and then he would get in trouble with Sylvie and, if Richard was home, him too.

Richard was not a likeable man. Well, my mother didn't like him. He was Sylvie's husband and often spoke condescendingly to her and I think that he liked her modest intellect because of the power it gave him. He controlled all of the money, and it was very much as though Sylvie was another of his children. Richard's preferred procedure for punishment for the boys was abetted by a leather belt which hung over the bannister at the top of the stairs. He was a Christian, too.

After I left Sylvie's, I didn't see her again for a long time. It was perhaps fifteen years later when I saw her in the supermarket.

She was so small. She had always been small, but looked almost ridiculously small to me now. I hugged her and she felt like a child. She barely recognized me, but she looked just the same if with a few more grey hairs. She spoke fondly of our time together and I asked her about the boys, and about Richard. Richard was not well at all. We talked about the other kids and the way they tormented Mark. And then Sylvie said that Mark would ask her when can we just be a family again? The boys didn't want to share their mum with other kids. And I didn't want to sit waiting in someone else's house for my own mum. How can anyone get it right?

I told my mother that I had seen Sylvie and we spoke a while about those times. She said that she knew she had found the right person to look after me. And I suppose she had, only I had been looked after by the wrong people for my whole life until then. Trial and error. We spoke about the little girls, little Molly and little Heather, and I told my mother about the mean things that I had done and said. Unexpectedly, my mother said that she already knew. In fact, she said, Sylvie had told her. She had said I think that Catherine is being cruel to the little ones. And then for the first time, I felt guilt – or was it shame? How are you meant to go through life not knowing what people really think until you find out years later and your heart breaks and your whole understanding is betrayed?

Sylvie was a saint. She said that I was like her daughter. She had always wanted a girl.

SWISHY WASHY

I pretend that I am a big girl but the dark is scary. Me and James sit behind Bernard and everything is black. Everything is black or maybe it is nothing. Then the thunder starts. I feel around, my tiny hands on seat and on legs and on door. I cannot see at all apart from a little stripe of James's face. He looks scared too and that makes me feel better. He is always more scared of things than I am. It is loud. So loud that I can barely even hear Bernard's booming voice. But I still can. He laughs. The big wings come over us and the sea pours over our heads but we do not get wet. Trapped in the dark and the loud dry wet. It feels as though the black roof above us will fall in, but everything is black now anyway. Is there no end to the black and the noise? The urr urr urr. Slapping and smashing against the black around us and the black being smeared with white suds. Teeth and tongues scraping and rubbing and wiping all over. I put my head down into my hands and my tiny hands are smaller even than my tiny head. I try to cover my face and get as small as I can so that I don't get chewed all up and spat on like the spitting all over sloshy all in its belly. For once I want to be small. There is spit everywhere. The windows drip with spit. I shield myself from it but none of it touches me anyway. It feels as though it should come through the windows but it does not. Me and James sink into the soft black that is beneath us. We look at each other as if for the last time and I am not sure that would be such a bad thing. The softness is better than the thunder and the monster above. Laugh laugh laugh Bernard goes. This has sometimes happened with Mum but she does not laugh she gives us ice lollies and tells us it will be okay. Will it? I keep thinking when will this big monster just eat us already? When will I drown? I don't know how long it is, but after a while, one of those long whiles, the light is there again and the still black car rolls out onto the still black street. And Bernard laugh laugh laugh as the car gets further away from the rotten black and the swishy washy red yellow and blue. Laugh laugh and shut your eyes but it doesn't go away. Loud and dark like the cinema that very first time when I thought it was what I wanted but it was scary and it was too late. I thought it was what I wanted but it wasn't. That old familiar feeling. It always goes on too long. The swishy washy always too long. The laugh laugh laugh. And he says that wasn't so bad was it?

SANDWORM

It was a sandworm like from that film. Or a mouse. A worm with no face and no eyes. And it moved like a fat lazy worm. I think it was dead and hands moved its lifeless body around. I know what it looks like but I don't think it is from memory. And I can see it so closely, in my eye line, but also from up above. Flopping around, the dead sandworm. The headless mouse. Lolling about like it was made of jelly. What was it? I have always been scared of jelly. I don't like not knowing what's going on. I don't trust anyone. I think I am a good judge of character.

UPSTAIRS

I can see out of a window but not right in front of me. It feels early in the morning. I don't know whether I have a drink or not, and if I do, what is it? Orange cordial? Or water? Or nothing? I don't think I ever had drinks at Bernard and Pat's. The room is not big. Today is different. I don't think that I've ever been in this room before. It is so quiet. It is quiet a lot when I am here. The telly only seems to be on when James is here. Today he is not. The radio might be on in another room but I don't think so. Maybe it is on in this room. It is so hard to see, to hear. The sun does not pour but, rather, drifts through the tree outside and then through the window into the room. The window is open and it is cold. The door is behind me and it is shut. Table and me. I sit at table and in front of me I can see my hands and all of my pens, all of the colours. My paper too. There is nothing in this house for children. Apart from the Lego that day, I suppose. And now I think, and I can remember that cupboard under the stairs. I remember the smell of that cupboard. It smelled like a cupboard. The whole house smelled like that cupboard. The door was the size of a real door. My memory seems different to everyone else's. I try to I try and try and I can't. I remember the paper well. It is part of a letter writing set and is blue and has little Dalmatian dogs on it at the top like a stamp. Today I am writing letters. I could be writing to my auntie Sandra who lives far away near the sea, or I could be writing to my godmother Anna. I am on my own and time goes by very slowly. I was never very good at telling the time and it made me feel ashamed. Even when I grasped a basic understanding of it, still for years, I had to have a watch with numbers on. Or I had a digital watch for a long while. I don't know how my letters ever reached their recipients. Perhaps they never did. I wander out of the room and shout Pat. She is the only one here. She is in a room. I stand on the landing and shout her. She comes out and tells me go back and do your letters. I sit and gather all of my pens together in colour order. I never play with dolls but sometimes I use my pens as people. My favourite colour is orange, so orange pen is the most good person. Pink is my most worst colour and pink pen is the most bad person. I make all of the other colours join in while orange is mean to pink. I make them argue and orange wins and none of the other colours like pink. Orange says pink nobody likes you and then orange and the others all leave pink on its own. I am orange. This lasts for a while. I rock on the chair and I rearrange my things on the table. I do get up to wander around the room occasionally but I have to be careful so as not to make any noise because I am scared Pat will come in and I will get in trouble. I get scared and jump back to my seat every few seconds. Time is different. A minute feels like days. I had no gauge of the passing of time either. There was a time on holiday once when we were on the bus. Mum and James and Uncle David and Auntie Bet (who was actually Mum's auntie and not mine) and I, again. Uncle David said to me I bet you can't stay quiet for a whole five minutes. And I said yes I can. And after what must have been about forty-five seconds I said has it been five minutes yet. I cannot wait any longer. I get up and I open the door quietly and I sit on the landing at the top of the stairs. I lean on the bannister and sit on the step sideways. I am not allowed this high up. Why is it different today? I sit for a while and it is just as boring out here. There is never anyone else. I get used to being alone and knowing that Mum is the only one who can change it. Then a noise and my head flings back, facing straight up. Pat stands over me and she says what are you doing go back in there. I think that she is busy ironing.

BIRTH

Mum said that when I was about six I came to her crying. She said what is wrong? What has happened? And I said Mum I don't want to have a baby. Mum laughed with relief. You don't have to worry about that yet. But Mum I said it will hurt. How do you know? Mum said. I don't know.

SPORTS DAY

Another sports day and I won and you weren't there. I won I promise but you'll never know for sure.

BERNARD

Bernard was like a big bald clown. He made jokes all of the time. He did also sometimes shout. His voice boomed like a giant's. His voice was very loud but he wouldn't stay angry for long. I would stay upset for much longer. He was very tall and always had stubble on his face, it was white. Northern accent but the odd word sounded posh. His voice was loud. He always joked and he sat down a lot too. He sat in the slouchy leather sofas. His face always looked like it was about to tell a joke ... A joke is a lie is a joke is a lie is a joke. It is all fun and games. I can't remember why he would shout at me. Then he would ask me what I was crying for. Boom boom, wotyucryinfoh. Tall, ogre. Big man. Rings on his fingers and in his ears and necklace around his neck. Which is odd isn't it. Dad didn't wear a necklace or earrings or rings. Beard and a big nose. Bald head. Huge ears, bigger and longer than any I'd seen but not bigger than his head. They would flap about. Stubble or beard all over his mouth and chin. His neck had stubble on it too and hung like a turkey's or as if he had eaten too much and was storing the excess there for the winter. It was always winter. Forehead wrinkled into his head so that I wasn't sure where one finished and the other started. Glasses, baggy t-shirts and a white long-sleeved shirt. I remember the white top more than the others. Loose pants jogging bottoms jeans. Flapping sandals with socks underneath them or sometimes no socks. I hated seeing his big feet and his toes. Hair creeping out, sandal creeping hair. I never saw him dressed smartly. Though you must have been that one day. must be the jogs

KITCHEN

I am sat in another room that I cannot remember at all. The table and the chair appear to be child sized but then I think again and it is adult size. I don't understand. I want to remember the cupboards but I can't. This whole house that I spent so long in is fuzzy and fragmented but it is this room that continues to elude me most curiously. What happened there? I tear my tiny head apart for answers, and I shake it, remember, remember you stupid little idiot why can't you do anything? I can see Bernard and Pat stood in the room doing things and moving around and the light is a yellowy light. Can't you see? Garlic never made Dad better. There was no garlic at home; there was only bland food at home. Smiley faces. After Dad died, and maybe before, James and I were always allowed to eat whatever we wanted. Mum would ask what do you want for tea and I would say and Mum would ask James what do you want for tea and he would say and she would make our separate teas, and afterwards she would make something different again for herself. Why would children be allowed this kind of power? Maybe this is why James is so spoiled. Kids are made to eat their tea, and especially their veg, or no pudding. I had no veg. I had pudding if I wanted pudding. I had sweets before tea. I had whatever I felt like. I think Mum thought that she should give us whatever we wanted for tea because Dad had died. But I didn't know what garlic was. I'd rather have known what garlic was than any of the teas that I picked.

TRICKY KNICKERS

Bernard used to call me tricky knickers because I was so bright. Was I? I wore yellow and orange a lot. And my small face had such an innocence to it. I had so much faith in people and in life, but all I can say is that it has gone and gone and gone over the years. Bernard used to call me tricky knickers because I was so bright. Bright, I have come to learn, is always thought of as tricky. For all the good it has done me, it has done so much wrong. I always work against myself. And people don't like bright. Bright is difficult, tricky. Bright is trouble. As I got older, I would wish to my mum that I could be stupid. I would say that the stupid kids at school were so happy and carefree. And I said that being smart is meant to be a good thing but I am sad and they are happy. And wouldn't it be nice to be blissfully ignorant. And do I really know so much more? Am I better off? By the time I got to high school, the verdict was split: half of the teachers liked me because I was smart, and the other half thought that I was a smartarse and resented me. It would be easy for me to say that the latter were half-witted miscreants but then it would also be true. Bernard used to call me tricky knickers because I was so bright. Bernard had lots of nicknames for me. He was that kind of man. He was silly all the time unless he was angry. He used to have so many different names for me it was as if he didn't like my real name. Most of the names used to end in knickers. I don't remember what my knickers were like but I must have worn them to have all of those knickers names. Bernard used to call me tricky knickers because I was so bright my mum said.

JAMES

James and I wrestled a lot. We watched wrestling on telly and would recreate the moves. James derived great pleasure from choke slamming me into the sofa. This drove my mum to distraction, but then she let us watch the damn thing in the first place. It was on late at night and was inappropriate. What did she expect? You will pay for that sofa if it gets broken! she would say, a threat that held little weight. One day there was a story in the newspaper about a young girl who had died after her brother had tombstoned her into their sofa and broken her little neck. We stopped doing tombstones after that.

As we got older and through puberty James developed problems with managing anger. The fun wrestling stopped and his horrible, violent, emotional outbursts replaced it. He had a tough time of it with no man around to show him how to be. And I knew the exact words to say in order to hurt him; but then I was the one who would be hurt. He went through a phase where he could not control his rage and would lash out very physically. I, obviously younger and smaller, didn't stand a chance. One time he pinned me down into that sofa and punched me repeatedly in the face until he was dragged off by my poor mother screaming that she would kick him out. Obviously, she would never have done anything of the sort.

I think back to these times and I feel for him. I think back to nicer times, too. Mum had bought a big new telly and James and I used the empty box as a cinema to watch it in. In those days, we went to the video shop every week to get films. This week, we chose *Dumb and Dumber* as our film. James and I sat in the box and watched it every day until the videos had to go back.

MONSTERS

I was sitting in the hall and the hall was dark. The front door had thin strips of windows in it, a row at the top and a row at the bottom. I could only reach the bottom ones but I would sit and press my forehead and my nose against the cold glass and make it wet and it was always wet already even though it was inside. You couldn't see out of it. It had lines in it that went from the bottom to the top. I could see lights and I could hear noises outside and I would wait every day until I could hear the car drive up and the car door close and Mum's legs coming down the path. I have spent my whole life waiting. Waiting for Mum. Waiting for Dad. Waiting for something bad to happen. I was sitting with my face on the glass in the dark and I liked the feeling of the cold on my cheeks and my squished nose. But this time, this dark evening as I sat, the living room door slammed shut behind me and I heard the lock click even though I don't think that the living room door ever had a lock. It was locked now. Now there was no light at all, not even coming through the gap underneath that door, and I couldn't see anything. I tried to move around in the hall but I could not see and I fell and fell and I fell. I fell until I just lay still on the floor so that I wouldn't fall any more. I tried to look up at the ceiling but it wasn't there. There was only dark everywhere.

Something had its hands over my eyes and it was a monster. It pressed its hands over my eyes and I couldn't have seen it anyway in all the dark. It had come from the cupboard under the stairs. It covered my eyes and it said into my ears no one is ever going to pick you up. I could feel its horrible breath on my horrible ears as it said no one is ever going to pick you up and it breathed and it breathed. I was scared but it didn't feel like when I was scared in bed at night. When I would go and get in bed with Mum and that one time I got in bed with Dad on the wrong side, because of the dragons. No it didn't feel like scared normally felt. I just lay still and I didn't want to move my hands or my mouth or my legs or anything. I didn't even cry cry. I just lay still and listened to the monster and felt its horrible breath and its horrible hands. And after a while the monster left and went back into the cupboard under the stairs. But it didn't stop saying no one is ever going to pick you up and I could still hear it. And I can still hear it now.

LADIES

I asked my mother if she remembered anything strange happening during those years. Asked if she remembered anything strange about Bernard. She said no. But then she said, well there was once. She told me that I had come home one day and told her about a book I had looked at with Bernard, a book that had pictures of ladies with no clothes on in it. I asked her what she thought, what she did. She said that she had called Pat straight away and she told her what I had said and that Pat didn't know what to say and that she was so shocked and that she cried. You cry now, Pat. Cry cry. My mother said that Pat told her that she would have to go off the phone and speak to Bernard about it. She couldn't believe it. Pat then arranged for my mother to go to speak with her and Bernard. Mother went to see Pat and Bernard at their house the next day and sat and had a talk with them and Bernard said. Oh Bernard. Bernard said oh it's so silly he said I was looking in a catalogue for birthday presents for Pat he said and I was looking at the underwear and the dressing gowns and the nightwear for her and Catherine wanted to help choose he said! Oh Bernard laughed! How silly, how funny! Oh little Catherine has ruined the surprise now! It all seemed innocent enough. It all seemed silly, seemed like a silly misunderstanding, of course. Kids say the darndest things. I don't remember the book. My mother never told Dad what had happened, there was no use in it, and I carried on going to Bernard and Pat's until I was about eight. My mother: here was a woman who had spent her childhood years going to bed at night fearing not monsters but that her mad mother might throw herself out of the window while she slept. How the mind lulls us. How we strive to ignore the worst possibilities. Oh Mother, how you have strived to lead a normal life. I love you. I love you so much. We cursed ladies, we never had a hope in the world. Pat were you really so blind? Or were you scared too? You, cursed too?

DAD

I have this dream and he rams your Christian cross down your throat you phony. Rips that chain from around your thick red neck. You slack-necked snake. You're a toad. Your red neck even redder now with blood that cuts through into the pattern of those treacherous links. Gold. Everything was gold. You know what, it might have been silver. You were a cheap man's flash. You turkey. Dad rips that chain off and he throws it on the ground, yes. Holy Dad. He could never be you. You piss over good men like my father. And why can't I remember any of it. The word piss makes me feel this sickly kind of familiarity when I think of you. Have I poisoned myself? Or was it you? When I had no chance to begin with. Did you ever think about that? Do you ever think at all? Oh yes you did. Cunning Christian. You made me old. No, Dad could never be you. He would save me from you. He would have. I can see you so well. See your neck, so red from shaving, with spots and tiers and layers straight into your loose chin. How could you look at him? How could you look at my perfect dad your cross shining against his. How do you laugh straight in the face of faith? Spoil everything that is pure and true and innocent? No Dad to save me. Maybe I'll kill you myself. You fat neck. Bernard.

DANIEL

Daniel is Laura's brother. They are adults now, but I suppose I am too. They have been adults for longer than James and I. They had more time. Daniel nearly died when he was twenty because he was an alcoholic and one of his funny friends put him in a wheelie bin and threw it into the sea and he began to choke on his own vomit. Nobody talks about it now. Daniel got all the girls then. He had a succession of glamorous girlfriends, though in truth they were all common. My family: my mum and my uncle, my aunties and Uncle Jon, would all laugh and they would joke that I fancied Daniel. I was a child. I hated it then, and when I think about it now I just find it disturbing and strange and I hate it still. What a strange joke. He is my cousin. He is now a normal man with an ugly and lazy wife and two small children. He works hard and gets little in return. He is casually racist. His father is an alcoholic too and I imagine that they'll both die of it. His father is the one who always sang that song to me. My mum helped him in his drunken stupor to sell a house or something, and in return he sent her some flowers and a £200 gift voucher. My mum said that it was too generous. I told her he's not generous, he's drunk. My mum has always treated Daniel a bit like he is her son. His life has been uneventful and I imagined that it would stay that way, only now he needs a new heart. Dumb wife, job's gone, pig heart. Don't you want more Daniel? Is that all there is?

HOLIDAY

The only time that I wasn't there was when we were on holiday, and Mum said Bernard and Pat's cost even more money then. We went on lots of holidays when I was a child. I have been to every seaside town in Britain. And on these holidays I often saw Uncle Jon. He wasn't my real uncle, but he and Auntie Lyn had been together since before I was born. He kissed me when I grew up. That was on a holiday too. I was sixteen and he said he had waited as many years. He said I've waited sixteen years for this. You watched me grow up.

I told my mum and she said that I must have encouraged him. I cried and then she gave him a call at work for a little chat. She said that at first he pretended that he didn't know what she was talking about but then he cried too and he said but but but. My mum scared the life out of him, quite literally. I didn't see him, or my Auntie Lyn, for three years afterwards. I always felt bad for Lyn. Mum had begged me not to tell her sister the truth and though I didn't think it was right, I did it for her. Lyn didn't know, and so must have thought that I didn't want to see her. Recently, Jon left her for another woman. He looks like death. I imagine that the cancer will come for him soon. He used to grab my arms and hit me with them and say cath why you hitting yourself cath why you hitting yourself

Jon was tall. All of these men were so tall. The men in my life aren't tall any more. Dad would never treat me like this. Does that help? It's hard to tell. What is this feeling? This craving? Oh hurt. This intense need to be loved. So punishing. I hate you because you don't love me. And I continue to love you because you don't love me. I don't want this again. So again and again. Am I just desperate to be in control desperate to be the unloved so desperate to cling onto my dad that I cannot replace him with another man how dare I should I dare? And I think that I never get over any of these men because getting over them feels like losing. Feels like giving up, letting them win the fight. Letting them win. I feel like I can't forget the men, can't get over them, can't move on because I feel that to do that I would have to forget my dad, get over his death, move on with my life. And well I just haven't and it feels like I just can't and just never will. I have to love them to keep hold of Dad. if I let them go I let him go. Let it go let it go. Stop living in this horrible deluded made up past life. waake up.

I still think about all of the men who have come and gone. They all go. Now that I am older, the game has changed a little, and I always win. I win by not letting them in. My mother has started to believe that she can psychoanalyse me. I think you're just looking for a dad, she says. No shit Mum.

YOU SILLY GIRL

How do we see? My optician told me that I have better than 20/20 vision. But when I was a child, I don't think that I could see at all. I couldn't see the future and I couldn't see anything, and now, I cannot see the past. If I could go back and if I could have seen then maybe all would not be lost. I can't see through my eyes only through a lens that someone else seems to hold. It feels like I live my life this way. I don't want to. I would if I could. I would if I was allowed to. My little eyes swell up with wet again in my little head. Little wet eyes again like a little cat. And I think about that young day and that green grass. Colours meant more. I walked into the big pointy place with my mum and she was crying a lot. Everyone had stood outside and then everyone had gone in. It was cold in there. The seats were in lines like at the cinema but they were not comfy. It reminded me of Christmas and singing and oranges and my aunties and uncles. I looked to the end of the room and there was Dad lying in a blue bed with tubes coming out of him. Hello Dad! I remember that he was asleep when he looked like that, Mum said. We walked

95

along and I let go of Mum and I walk and I ran towards Dad and he was so far away and it seemed that he kept getting more far away and my legs hurt and they were tired. All of the grown ups sitting on either side of me watched and they cried and smiled and cried more. What a funny thing to do. There was Auntie Bet and Lyn and Jon and David and Granddad and Auntie Bet and Lyn and Jon and David ... Granddad makes me cry. He made me cry much later when he looked so much like Dad and hugged me with a kind of hug that I could never manage to imagine or feel and he made me cry cry when he died. I got closer and I was going to tell Dad about the paints at dinnertime and the car and and. Then Bernard was there. Bernard stood in front of Dad. And I stopped there on that long road and my stomach bit itself all over. My hands clenched my yellow dress up into a big crunchy clump. And I could taste my little belly and now that swelled instead of my eyes. Only they swelled too. And the salty that came from my eyes went into my mouth and mixed with all the sicky. I sat on the floor in my dress and my little legs lay flat out. My sore legs. My dress was still scrunched up and my shameful little knickers were on show. And I pressed my dress onto my wet face in my little hands and I cried and I hid my face like I always did so that by the time I had uncovered it everything would have gone away. But the sick was coming again. I pushed my little bit of yellow dress into my mouth to stop it but it was no good. The dress came out along with all the sick. I sick up and up all over my little dress and I'm crying and everyone is looking at me and Bernard is talking and everyone is looking at him and saying how beautiful and everyone says what a lovely man and everyone says so thoughtful. And I am being sick and sick and sick. And I try to say stop but I am just sick again. Instead of words there is just sick. I lie on my front to push my little belly in and to get rid of the swelling gunge but it comes out anyway and I lie with my chin and my body lay down in the now thrashing waves of sick. My hands are so small and I can see them clutching onto the floor so innocently and it is so unfair. My body moves almost like a bug a caterpillar being sick and being sick again. And then my belly hurts and no one ever will do anything. Bernard says JIM JIM JIM and my tongue rolls out of my mouth. JIM and I can feel my cheeks and my throat begin to fold back over my face. My little nose and my wet eyes have gone and the sick is now pushing my whole body inside out. I am lay a dead pile of sick and mess and child and at least we're both dead and I can see now. I can see now. And I didn't know where I was or how I got there I just was there and you or someone or something made me need to be a grown up, because grown up is when everything is better and okay, but I wasn't and it wasn't and it isn't. I wasn't allowed to be dirty.

SAM HINES

A few years later, and my first proper kiss. Sam didn't have a dad either, but his family was poorer than mine. He lived in a scruffy house and he was bad. I pretended to be bad but I wasn't at heart. He wasn't smart enough to be good. I had principles and I was scared of things. He didn't seem scared of anything. Sam's mother couldn't control him whereas I still felt a sense that my mum should be obeyed. I still felt a sense of not wanting to get into trouble. Sam almost thrived off the prospect. We were in school, I think maybe the last year of junior school. People had started kissing. The kids would gang together to force a boy and a girl to kiss if it was suspected that they fancied each other. Bushes lined the yard and you could kind of get inside them. My group of friends and I hung out inside them. And when it was decided that a boy and a girl were going to kiss, they would be sent into the bush to do it while the others waited outside. I liked Sam and I guess he liked me, but I didn't really want to go into the bush. The others chanted and jibed and spurred and there was no other option than to do it. My friend Ellie had already kissed J.J. Greatbanks in the bush, and they were now going out. I actually liked J.J. better than Sam. He was smart and we were good friends. But I did like the danger of Sam. I've always gone for the wrong ones. So, we went into the bush and we hunched for a few moments under the branches discussing whether or not we should just do it. And then we did it. Sam's mouth was cold and wet and he shoved his slimy tongue into mine. It was disgusting. But I felt glad to have done my first kiss. Sam and I kissed a lot after this. He used to come round to my house and we would go up to my room to watch a film but instead we would kiss messily and stupidly for hours. I remember that during one of these sessions we fell off my bed and knocked the lamp from my bedside cabinet to the floor, caught up in the eyes tight shut rapture of wet snogging. My mother ran up to see what was going on and we gave some kind of desperate excuse for the noise. But, when we emerged from the bush that first time, the others didn't even believe that we had kissed. It was all for nothing. Later, Sam and I were to go to the same high school and we promised to remain boyfriend and girlfriend. Only, after the first week he met a blonde girl who had come from another junior school and told me that he was going to go out with her instead.

DOG

Dad won us a giant dog teddy at a fair once. It was a big white dog, like the one from *The NeverEnding Story* and James and I would sit on it and pretend to fly. Mum hated it and it was soon sent up to the loft. It was too big she said.

For me, the loft incited both terror and excitement. It was damp and the roof was low, it was not suitable for renovation like in some people's houses. The loft usually meant Christmas, which was my favourite time of year, but then it was dark and scary and full of spiders. We kept all of the decorations up there and I would always want to help get them. Occasionally while we were up there, my mum or Uncle David would go down the ladder back into the house and I would be left up there alone and I would become immediately terrified and want to get out.

There was and still is a bamboo stick with a metal hook that we used to pull the ladders down for the loft. I liked the taste of the metal and would sit on the sofa with the hook in my mouth and the stick sort of propped up by the floor. My mum would shout at me to get that thing out of my mouth but I did it again and again when she wasn't looking. One of these days my hands slipped and I cut the roof of my mouth open with that tasty hook.

The dog didn't stick around for long, and I imagine it ended up in the arms of another child one happy Christmas after being sent to the charity shop – that godforsaken place. Mum got a real dog for us after Dad died. Really, it was for James. Mum said that she got it to guard the house, but she got it to help James overcome his fear of dogs. Next door had an Alsatian, and its loud barking scared him to death. We got a Jack Russell, a tiny little wretch with no hope of guarding anything. Mum and James named it Patch – the name of a cat we had previously. I didn't understand why you would reuse a name for a different pet. Patch the cat had died and now we had Patch the dog. I immediately disliked Patch the dog after she shat down the leg of my school trousers and into my white sock, and I disliked her still when she died a couple of years ago. She lived too long.

She had to be put down a couple of years ago. Mum did not want to be in the room when it happened. Instead she wanted me to be there. She did not want to see or want to look, but she wanted someone to see. For my mother, I guess, it was easier to look away. The dog still died. I told my mother that Patch drifted peacefully into an everlasting sleep. The reality of the case was very different. She did not look peaceful. In fact, she shook violently, urinated involuntarily, and bit through her own pink bacon tongue. If Mum did not want to look, then I thought it appropriate, too, to hide the truth from her. She did not want to see, would not want to know.

When my own cat was put to sleep earlier this year, I knew that I had to see. For me, the forever-unanswered questions that would accompany not seeing outweighed the sadness of the experience. And after witnessing Patch's experience, I would not leave my prince alone. My mother could not understand my decision. As I had questioned her decision to look away, she questioned my decision to see. It made no sense to her. She never wants to see at all because seeing makes things real.

It was, in fact, much more 'peaceful' for Muk. I held him and he looked into my eyes as he gently fell out of consciousness. The vet had talked through the procedure very frankly with me, as she must have gathered I would want. She told me that he would first become sedated to unconsciousness, and only after this would his heart stop beating. It was over quite quickly. His sad lifeless body felt much heavier than before, with no effort of his own to hold himself up. His eyes were still open. He looked alive. It was hard to imagine him dead when he still looked so alive.

It was only after he had died that it became something to look away from. I went to pass him to the vet when brown fluid poured out of his tiny nostrils with such great force and he emptied out like a pyjama bag. Due to the illness that caused his death, his stomach had filled with this fluid and now it was being expelled. I could have been horrified – perhaps I was or should have been. And too, I was in a state of nothingness. But I concentrated on the fact that this scene validated my more horrifying decision:

that he could not have lived with all that brown stuff. Could not have lived a bloated misery. He was so beautiful. And this rationale permitted him to remain beautiful through all of the horror and the gunge. My innocent boy. I had done the right things, if there are ever such things.

LORD

Bernard only turned to God a few years before I was born. I wonder which way he had turned up until then. He once said on a video you could say that I lived a life which I wasn't proud of. I wonder what he meant.

HEATHER

You, the first little Heather. I don't know if you had a dad either. I liked you and I hated you. Everyone cared about you and no one cared about me. But for a time at least you were something to play with. Something to talk to. Not always alone any more. Your mum is Pat's daughter. I wonder if she is alive. She had the same sneery snarled up face as Pat. I don't think she liked me very much at all. Maybe she knew that I could be mean to you. I was, whenever I wanted. Whenever you wouldn't do as you were told. I went to your house once, her house. You live in a poor house, those houses with no gaps between them and the door opens right onto the street. I think Bernard and Pat were busy or maybe they didn't want to see me because instead of being at their house they took me to your house. Your house full of toys and so pink. Teletubbos. Tubby toasty. Hoover. There wasn't room to move your toys were everywhere and your house smelled. I think they came to pick me up again later or I think your rude mum drove me back there. I don't know if I told my mum about it. You are blonde and I saw you years later, more grown but not grown up. I felt jealous of you, and I always had. You seemed to have a purity and a sense of a chance that I was never allowed. So blonde little curly girl. I didn't want to be mean but I had to it was all I had. You, like all the rest, had everything.

MUM

I've got to tell you Mum that I don't blame you. I don't blame you for any of it. Your poor life. Listen to me go on. Couldn't it have been different for you? And people like Bernard and Pat, Mr and Mrs Twit, they find people like us Mum. The cursed. They always will. You are everything. You better believe it. How quickly the clock will tick when the curtains fall. Or, god forbid, how slowly. But didn't you have a feeling? Didn't you wonder?

BRICK

The house isn't painted but it is now. I have painted it. Its walls were a muddy brown brick brick brick but now I have painted it and it is black. There are no white lines between the bricks, they are black. The bricks that were all their own shade of mud are now black. And the windows that I could never see into and I could never see out of anyway are black. The paint slid so nicely over those windows. And when I painted the door, thick black tar over the door, I painted the handle and the lock and I painted the edges and the seal so you won't be leaving ever again. Like I never leave. The door is painted shut and your house can stay clean forever and you can keep your shoes in the hall all of your life. And you can sit on the floor on your white carpet and you can sit by the door and press your face against it all you want because no one will ever come and pick you up. Don't you dare go up those stairs. Get down from there. Don't you think I remembered? The doors to all of those rooms that never existed anyway are all black too. You are not allowed up there. And the kitchen, that is black. The kitchen that is always black in my head. Oh and those sofas are so so black. Those white sofas are so black, can you imagine? You don't have to. Why don't you go and sit on them? Because they are the only things you will ever sit on again. Are they comfy? You wondered why I was upside down, well I can see the sun and I know I can make it but all you will ever see is black.

FAIR

One day Dad took James and me to a fair. There is a photo of us. Dad took photos all the time, and so now I have a strange collection of memories that don't really exist and millions of snapshots of myself as this innocent little child and of this man that I have never met. I have these photos on display all around my flat. It is a strange thing that people do. I wonder if you would still take photos, Dad. Wonder what you would make of me. Would I make you proud? I suppose that I would be different if you were here. Everything would be different. In the photo at the fair Dad holds me in one arm and James stands in front of his legs. I have a big scab on my nose and an unfair haircut. Mum said that I must have fallen over. But I am smiling. I smile in all of the photos. The cut on my nose in this photo looks a lot like the birthmark that remains on my neck to this day. The doctor said it would go by the time I was five. Mum called it a Strawberry. It was funny, because I went to a place called Strawberries while Mum was at work sometimes. They said little strawberry with a little strawberry! I hated that name. It made me embarrassed. Nowadays I find it hard to hate anything. The birthmark never went away and after a while we stopped asking when it would. It was meant to go when I was five, but I guess Dad went instead. Dad took us to the fair and he was wearing a silly shirt and blue jeans. We went on the bouncy castle but then James got stung by a wasp and he cried and I had to come off the bouncy castle and we had to go home. I cried, too. But not for James. I cried for myself.

RULER

You couldn't draw a straight line with a ruler Bernard said. But it wasn't my fault. Is anything? Is it a saying, that? He made it sound like a saying.

This adage troubled my life in later years. I went to school and they all said it too. Mrs Prescott walked around the class. It was English, my favourite. She walked around to take a look at what we were all doing. When she reached me she was visibly appalled. I had been writing away and the whole page was nearly full! Only, all of the words sloped diagonally instead of sitting neatly along the lines of the paper. Awful! she said. You need to improve your presentation Katy, awful! I was hurt, of course. Words are always powerful but for children they are razors.

My first teacher in that school was called Miss Mitchell. She was okay. She was extremely nasal. She looked like a rat. One of the things that we did in her class was a sandwich project. I am not sure why this was on the curriculum but it produced one wholesome time for little Catherine. I was seven. We all spent several weeks putting together a plan for a sandwich that we would then go on to make. Miss Mitchell told us to write about which ingredients we would use, and the process by which we would make the sandwich. We had to draw pictures of these ingredients, and of what we hoped or imagined that the resulting sandwich might look like. And then finally, the big day came. My mother had helped me to collect the necessary ingredients when we did the food shopping on the Sunday before. I always went with Mum to do the food shopping. I was so excited to make my sandwich, and with some great stroke of chance it turned out just as I had planned. The result? A ham, cress and carrot sandwich. But this is what happens when a child chooses ingredients. I can taste it now crunch crunch. We all had photographs taken with our sandwiches and we stuck them in at the end of our sandwich booklet to prove that we had made them. I was so proud. It is one of my fondest memories. I don't think that I have ever felt as proud since. I always did well in school, if I was interested in doing so. My achievements now don't have a scratch on the pride that sandwich instilled within me. It became harder and harder to feel satisfied. Now I only look to the next possible feat. Nothing is ever enough. I ate the sandwich.

There was a girl called Heba in Miss Mitchell's class and she was Indian. She was, in fact, the only Indian person that I knew. Her skin was a different colour to everyone else's. Growing up in the North West of England, the people that I met were predominantly white. Heba was very clever, and had the best handwriting in class. I thought this was because she was Indian. I was always jealous of her surpassing us all, surpassing me. She was allowed to use pen before anyone. I came next – but not good enough! Despite this,

I liked Heba a lot. I remember that as well as getting presents at Christmas and on birthdays, like everyone else, she also used to get them at other times because of special parties that her family had every year. Once, she brought in a fluffy white cat teddy and we all crowded around her to admire it. When I was about ten Heba told me that she had to move to Cardiff because her dad was a doctor and had secured a job there. I thought that Cardiff was in India for a long time afterwards, and I never saw Heba again.

Another teacher, Mrs Whittaker. She was younger, she had a bouncy blonde bob that curled round her chin. She was a cunt. I knew that she was one because my mother didn't like her either, though she never called her a cunt. She ended up marrying a cricketer and moving to Australia, or something ridiculous like that. I have since resolved that her destination was fitting with historical perspective. She was my class teacher for a whole year, say, when I was around nine. I had taken to sitting sideways at my desk, with the chair parallel to the edge, as opposed to tucked underneath. My paper, or book, would then also be sideways, and I would write sideways. I wrote within the lines! But I wrote sideways. It was just comfier that way. And it looked the way it was meant to look on the paper. Well, Mrs Whittaker didn't like this one bit. In fact, I think she disliked me generally. She once told my mother that I was a ringleader and a trouble-causer. She had it in for me. I recognized her in the miscreants that I later encountered at high school. One time, my friend Demi was feeling sick and I ran across the playground to Mrs Whittaker to say Miss Whittaker, Miss Whittaker, Demi is going to throw up! Because that is what you are meant to do when you are a child, and at school, you are meant to tell teachers when bad things happen. Demi is going to throw up! I said. And she said, pardon? So, I said it again, Demi is going to throw up! Pardon? she said. I didn't understand. Miss, I said, Demi feels really sick and she's going to be sick. She's going to what?

she said. She's going to be sick! I said. No, Catherine, she is going to vomit, she said. What kind of person gets pleasure out of pedantically correcting a small child, especially at the cost of another small child throwing up? These people should not be allowed to teach. That cunt had neither the skills nor values that it takes to be an educator. So, anyway, she said, Catherine, if you sit straight then you can put your book straight. But I didn't want to. I was comfortable. She would tell me this every day. I must have stopped doing it at some point. It wasn't worth it. The sad thing is that people like this will always win. It's easier to give up.

But why would Bernard say it to me? I was not at school, no. I don't know what I was doing. Drawing. It couldn't have been so important that I could have been wrong, could it Bernard? A child. I couldn't do anything right. And I will never believe that I can. Apart from that I do. I think that I can do things right but then I know that they must be wrong. Because that is what I have learned. There is a lot of value in learning. I want to believe. But instead I believe and do not believe at the same time.

I think about ruler, about my Ruler: Dad. King Dad. How was I meant to draw a straight line?

I can sit however I want now.

AWAKE

I was such a nice child. So loving. But Dad still died. And I still sat alone all those days. I think that the more I do good things for other people the more bad things happen to me. Does it count as a good selfless deed if you feel bad afterwards? My dreams now feel more real to me than waking life. When I walk down the street it feels like I am in a PlayStation game. I no longer jump when cars pass. I barely open my eyes any more. And everything I do is so contrived. So made up. So a mismatched scramble of those I emulate. So everyone else because I have no self. So everyone else that I am no one. Sometimes I feel that I should piss myself just to see if I wake up somewhere new. And it's like these pseudo-memories are the only things that are real. I don't think I ever even like anyone. Little loving Catherine cannot love now. I just become obsessed with them, become them. I need it all, I need to know everything so that I can be anything because I do not know what to be, not what I am. I am lost in a way that only children can feel. When the supermarket feels so big that you might never get out. Dad never came back

CAMELOT

When I was younger I thought that I was afraid of heights, scared of rides. My mum and my brother were. The school trip to Camelot was coming up and I felt sick with dread in the preceding weeks. The first ride that we came to was called Venom and it was a big snake ride. It was inside when most rides are outside. While we were waiting in line Sam took the Nike cap that I was wearing off my head and threw it into a restricted area. I can't remember how I got it back but I did. It was a treasured possession and can be seen atop my little head in many photographs. Later we went on a big blue ride called The Rack. I was scared enough already but my seat was broken and I hung upside down out of the seat thinking that I was about to die. In all likelihood I was probably just too small to fit properly.

At the end of the day all of our groups had to meet at the exit, near the gift shop. Only it wasn't the end of the day. Not 5.30 p.m. The teacher looking after our group was Miss Howard and she was extremely tall and gangly and her voice was booming and manly and she was a jobsworth. She had made sure we were at the exit by 5 p.m.

I asked Miss Howard if I could go to the gift shop while we were waiting for the others to arrive. We were so early, after all. The gift shop has always been my favourite part of anything. I think that I still feel the same. Huh.

No, everyone must stay together, she said. I suggested that we all go to the shop together. No, she said. It felt so unjust. I stood sulking and after a while another group arrived. It was Mr Foster's group. He was very tall, too. And he had a deep voice, too. He often did assemblies at school and he would get these strings of claggy spit between his teeth when he talked, all the while his enormous Adam's apple bobbed violently in his throat. It looked so uncomfortable. But Mr Foster was an incredibly kind man. I wonder what happened to him.

I walked over to Mr Foster and asked if I could go to the shop, being careful to make sure Miss Howard didn't catch me. He said yes, of course, and I ran off gleefully. Upon my return Miss Howard scolded me for undermining her authority and putting myself at risk. When someone tells you no, you don't ask someone else, she said. Well, it didn't seem that way. It seemed that it was exactly what you should do. Better yet, don't ask at all if you think that the answer will be no – an adage my mum condoned enthusiastically throughout my life. Miss Howard called me the Comprehension Queen when I had her for English.

LYN AND SANDRA

Lyn and Sandra are my aunties. They are blonde and glamorous and tanned with their fancy nails and they only wear white. Sandra always reminded me of Patsy from *Absolutely Fabulous*. Me and Mum used to watch it. Lyn and Sandra rolls off my tongue so easily because I have said their names together more than ever apart. It is sad that I see them as a pair and my mum as separated from that pair. I suppose that it is because of the distance. We never lived near them. But it was more like they never lived near us. There was more distance than the places. Mum could never leave could she? They are Mum's sisters but Mum's mum didn't leave them. Lyn and Sandra had a sunbed shop where they lived for a long time I think though I only remember it a little bit. It was all made out of black stuff and had the big machines in it and smelled funny. Not bad but just funny. They always wore white and they'd stand behind the counter with their blonde hair. I remember once when we were where they live I got a toy guitar with buttons on it that made noises. I stood outside of the sunbed shop and put my cap on the floor to collect money and played for the people. James was embarrassed. I was young and happy and wearing cycling shorts. There is a picture, and I think I remember. I look happy. Mum told me that Auntie Sandra once smashed a plant pot over her husband's head. I don't think I ever met him. Sandra likes scary films and we would have to get them from the video shop when she was here. I only got scared by one of them but was scared every night for a long time after but never said anything. I don't get scared any more. None of it's real. She kissed a man called Jesús when we were on holiday in Spain. My favourite was Sebastian because he loved me and used to give me orange juice and crisps. I loved him. Lyn used to be Doctor Hoffer sometimes and it scared me and James and she used to give me Chinese burns which I hated but I liked her. I don't know if Doctor Hoffer was real but she would put on a deep voice and pretend to be possessed. She once ran around after me at her house when we were visiting trying to spray me with something she said was for 'growing a bust'. I was embarrassed. She once bought me some denim wooden heels that my mum said were too high for a girl my age. I clopped around on the paving stones in the back garden and loved them. Lyn and Sandra's nails click clicky around like Mum's but seem to do it even more with their bracelets and things. I have lots of memories of Lyn and Sandra but not really any before Dad went. They are funny women. But it all just makes me feel really sad. Mum, Lyn and Sandra. Tough old birds. Lost souls.

NO

Was it you? You big bald disgusting clown. You fraud. Was it you who taught me not to say no? You who made it so that I could not say no? I think of all those times when I resisted and resisted and then I lay back and thought of nothing. Thought of no. Never said no. It's funny that all my life I've felt everyone has always said no to me, but I cannot say no, not at all. I'm so desperate for men to love me that I never think to say no. Don't have the option, the right. And how could I say no when you were in charge? You were the adult, I was the child. I did as I was told. I still do. I spend all of my time trying to defy what I am told but I am the biggest conformer of them all. Master conformer. Yes man. Aim to please. I so long to please. All I want is for you to like me. How disgusting. For them all. To love me. So many adults, so many men, many dads, many people in charge, have taken advantage of their power. Why would I say no when I cannot. Don't answer back, can't. You won't love me if I say no and I hate myself for saying yes. Don't even say yes. Can't say anything at all.

MONKEY

When I was a child I had a teddy monkey, which I called Monkey, or Muk for short. It had been my brother's at first. But when I was christened someone bought me an expensive teddy called Rusty and James wanted it so we swapped. Muk wasn't expensive, he was just a normal teddy. I took him everywhere with me. I didn't play with dolls but I would put him in a toy pram and push him around instead. While I was still very young, I started to get these funny feelings that felt like needing a wee only different. I found that if I lay flat down on my face and held Muk down underneath me near the feelings, and rubbed up against it, it would feel nice. It was something about getting the pressure right. I would do it secretly whenever I could. But one time, my mother caught me. It felt like the worst thing in the world and I was ashamed. She said what the hell are you doing. You shouldn't be doing things like that at your age. And anyway, that's not how you do it. You do it differently and only when you are older. I still did it but I never got caught again.

BIRTHDAY

Waking up early in the morning in the winter, when it is still dark out, always reminds me of my birthday. It is in January. I am reminded of one specific birthday in particular. I think it was my seventh or eighth, but I could be wrong. James and I shared a room at the time. It was a school day and Mum hadn't even opened the curtains because it was still so dark, instead we had our bedside lamps on and it didn't seem like morning at all. I still had to go to school, but I got to open my presents on my bed first. Mum brought them in and I was excited. Mum went out to get something else but, to my surprise, upon her return she handed it to James. She had bought James a small present too, she explained, so that he didn't feel left out. And with that, my presents were stripped of all worth and meaning. It was my birthday, why should James get anything? I never got anything on his birthday. He got a gumball machine and he always got everything. Because my birthday is in January, I have always received sale presents, and this has remained the case to the present day. James was born in June and so he always receives proper presents. When I was born, my mum gave him a toy fire engine and said that I had brought it for him so that he would like me. I remember he once hit me over the head with it.

NEVER CARE

Big dead Dad. What does it mean? I expect you to come back one day like I expect them all to come back. When will I know better? Know you better? Other people want other things but I only want them to stay. Through thick and thin. And it's always so thin. Never care. I think I choose them this way. Choose the not care. Play out my story over and over. I think I feel it all but maybe I feel nothing. I understand nothing. Why can't I see? I swear that you could smash my desperate little head in and I would just Sellotape the pieces back together in the hope that I could look good again for you. In the hope that during the reconstruction I might have acquired some new and lovable qualities. Didn't I inherit anything from you dead Dad? Didn't I get anything from you? Your kindness or your good heart? Your suspension of judgement, your carefree tolerance. You brought them all together, oh you did. They all looked up to you dead Dad. You were so tall. All I do is make them go away. They always go. If they ever come at all. You went Dad. Dad you are gone. You are dead. But I, I am alive. What kind of cruel joke is this? So alive, it's true. Oh, it's true. So much so that it doesn't make sense. These true things often don't.

KATY

I hated my name Catherine when I was little. Mum said I chose Katy to be like my friends who had names like Demi and Rosie and Sophie. I thought Catherine was posh. The other kids would laugh at me when a new teacher would say Catherine for the register.

People have always spelled Katy wrong. They'd say Katie or they'd call me Kate. Hate! Bernard and Pat always called me Catherine never Katy. I think I was too young, then. I can hear Pat's voice saying Katy but I don't think she ever did.

I guess that from a young age I learned that being myself isn't right, isn't enough. Catherine was never good enough. Catherine was always being told off. Created Katy, instead. Katy could be whoever you wanted her to be. Will be whatever you want. Whatever I think they want.

When I was in my early twenties there was a guy that said I was like a caricature of a person. He said the way everyone says your name, Katy, everyone knows you. And it hurt. And it hurt because he was right. Maybe I thought that if I changed then other things might change, too. Maybe thought that if I was different then people would love me.

My mum told me that once during a time when I was in therapy she and my brother were chatting and he asked her
When she is 'cured' what will she be like?

My brother wouldn't call me Katy and never has to this day. He calls me CAFF. Perhaps he knows after all.

TICKLING

Tickling is where you laugh and cry at the same time. It feels so horrible. And feels so horrible to be laughing when really you hate it. Tickling is a confusing feeling. It feels like a lot of things feel. Bernard makes me cry but he laughs and smiles and says it is okay. He says that I should smile. I don't know what to do.

LOST BOYS

but I can never hate you Dad. You who have caused so much pain. King of ku-ku-kuh-katy. Auntie Lyn's ex-husband used to call me that. He sang that old war song. K-K-K-Katy, Beautiful Katy, You're the only g-g-g-girl that I adore. When the m-m-m-moon shines, Over the cowshed, I'll be waiting at the k-k-k-kitchen door. No Dad, cannot forgive you and don't want to. You never did anything wrong. Neither did I. I've never felt wrong. It is those others that make me feel wrong. When people say those were the days I don't know what they mean. Sam Hines, Sam James's friend, Ryan Thorley, Daryl Horsefall, Ashley Wild, J.J. Greatbanks, the Bernards and much later the Uncle Jons. And all those that came after and will come again and again. It doesn't end. Oh men just stay away stay away and don't look back

Doctor and doctor and teacher teacher teacher oh you men you dadly dads you poor horrible awful warm men you men you cannot ever give me what I want

Move on to the next. I gave your nickname to someone else. I give the same ones to all of these guys. Do they mean anything to me or do they just mean something about me? I bet I know the answeeeer

I still run around telling everyone about the boy I like, as though I am a child. All my life I thought I'd change. But you see I haven't changed at all. Haven't moved, haven't become better, am not worse. Have lived frozen in time.

GIYOVUH

You picked me up from school every day but I don't remember that now. Can only remember nasal and booming voices. Can remember geddardovit and giyovuh and wosumattawiyeh. I remember that there were conkers in school, it seemed like all the time. We were on the little side of school then. Remember when I slipped and cut my little legs remember the pain so cold but so hot, so raw and stinging like I have never stung since. There was a ring of tree stumps on the sandhills and Demi and me were jumping from one to the other. Demi was my best friend but would leave me for a new girl in later years. Then Demi left the school and that girl became best friends with me. Always second best. The bell rang and Demi jumped down and ran and was so far away so quickly. I tried to jump to follow her but my pathetic feet slipped and I fell, straddling the stump and ripping the insides of my legs to shreds. My mother came to pick me up and we went to the chemist. She bought me a Lucozade and wrapped my legs up in bandages so that I looked like a snowman, and then she took me back to school that afternoon. Would collect conkers. Worry that bugs would come out of them. Girls did handstands on the hill but I couldn't do handstands. I couldn't do cartwheels either. My body has never been free. My little soul might have been. No, I was always pensive. I can never look back and see myself. The only thing I remember about being picked up by you is the shame of not being picked up by Mum. Not Dad. The other kids and their parents and me with no one.

HOLY

I saw Bernard once, twice, years later. It was at a church. I was thirteen or fourteen. I had started going to a youth group at this church at the end of our road. Incidentally, this was also Bernard and Pat's church. I had never seen them there. I went every other Friday night and in truth it was just because my friends went – it was something to do, and you didn't have to pay attention to the religious stuff. They tried to indoctrinate us with it in their loving, 'funky' way, but it was easy to ignore. There were sweets and there was football and arts and crafts. After a while I made friends with the Christian kids there. Some of them I had already known, but I'm not sure that I had known they were Christian. Some were more Christian than others. There was one girl, Lucy. Lovely Lucy. She was an angel, a deity. Glowing. She may have been the most devout of them all. She was so good. She was so pure, and kind, and good. I don't know what she saw in me, perhaps some dim, flickering light somewhere deep down there. I felt very protective of her, though she was older than me. She was so innocent, and I had the street wise of a non-believer, with a quick wit. She liked me tremendously, I'm not sure why. I wasn't pure, or kind, or good.

Through her I did briefly become more interested in taking the religious side seriously, and for a short time – perhaps a year or less – I attended the services on Sunday evenings. The evening services seemed more fun, and there were usually more young people there and more things going on afterwards. However, as time went on I also attended the morning services. I tried as I could to believe. I'd got it into my head that perhaps it was something I could believe in, and that perhaps I should believe in something. And in my young, arrogant way I had also adopted the ideology of not knocking something until I tried it. But you know, it wasn't for me. I didn't believe. It was one of the many things I've tried on in my life. I've learnt that I dress up like the people around me and play the role they'll want me to play. I'm an imposter.

Lucy believed so deeply. I remember one Sunday morning. It was bright, not hot or cold but pleasant. It may well have been my first morning service there at the church. I sat and I stood next to Lucy throughout. She was so pleased that I was there. Perhaps I was just a fixer upper. Perhaps she thought that she could convert me to the righteous path. Oh it hurts to write even speculatively marring words against her, even now, even all this time passed. She was not driven by motive. I listened to the songs, and I didn't know the words. I bowed my head when everyone else bowed theirs. I stood and sat on cue. And at one point, during a song, I turned my head to look at Lucy. I looked at her and her eyes were closed, and I don't think that I've ever seen such a vision of ardent faith. She looked as though she was not on this plane, but another, better and more peaceful one. Her face looked so beautiful. Pious. And it brought tears to my eyes to see someone so lost in love and belief and happiness. And I found it so admirable for her to have so much faith in something, when I had none in myself, or in anything.

I visited for Sunday dinner at Lucy's once. She lived in quite a posh house, it was large, I'm not sure where it was. Her family was so reverently Christian – I felt like a bad influence. Her grandmother was there. I was respectful, I ate the dinner, and then I was offered dessert – apple pie. I turned this down because I don't like cooked fruit – my life would be easier if I did. I was then offered rhubarb fool instead, a spanner in the works. More cooked fruit. I had not anticipated an alternative dessert. Due to my, still ongoing, awkward disposition, I knew that I could not turn down two options (one was bad enough) without risk of seeming rude. I reluctantly accepted the fool, and in doing so also accepted the role of the fool. The bowl of tepid, phlegm-like rhubarb soup appeared in front of me and I wished that I had never been born, and that I'd never come to this house, and that I'd never been so ridiculous as to think that everything might be okay, and I cursed my mother for my bland and inexperienced palate. I sipped tiny slurps of the stuff from my spoon for as long as I could before I felt I might vomit.

Later, on one of these days, these Sunday mornings, I went to the church and I attended the service, and was invited to dinner this time by a girl named Rachel. Rachel's house was not posh. Her mother was dead, and she lived with her nervous and lonely father in their meagre but loving little home. I think perhaps they had only turned to religion in order to match some meaning to their grief, but I could be wrong. I went to her house and we had dinner and it was nice, her father was a good cook. Rachel was fond of me. I made her laugh an awful lot, but her laugh sounded pain-ful – like when you cry so hard that you begin to cough. Nothing like the charming giggles of Lucy. She made me feel superior, which I liked. But on this day, there was an unexpected believer at church. At the end of that Sunday morning's service, we had seen – of all the people in the world to see – Bernard. Imagine the look on my face. Well, you wouldn't believe it but a smile was there. A big great smile, happy to see him. Excited! Not sadness, nor sicky, nor anger, nor cry – but happiness. Delight! O Bernard! O Lord! O Dad! Not Dad. Never Dad. I wanted to impress him. He was a man, if not anything else, after all. He was happy too. I cannot remember what we talked about. I explained to all of the church lot Bernard used to be my child minder can you believe it? Really? they said. Yes I said. Bernard and Pat I said. Although, Pat was not there. I think that the others cherished this new information. They liked me and they liked Bernard – and presumably Pat. Bernard and Pat were religious. It was all coming together. I was one of them, really.

But then Bernard said one of those kinds of things that he always used to say. It was so good and so safe and happy and finally and then he said it. Said something strange and it made me feel all funny inside and I felt as humiliated and hurt and cry as I had all those years ago. When Catherine was a baby, Bernard said, I used to change her nappy, and one time I had to use a butter knife!

Laugh laugh laugh. Everyone laughed and laughed. Josh and Rachel and Michael and Lucy and Matt and Louise and all of their stupid laughing faces. They laughed at my name, they laughed at my shit, they laughed at me. Laugh laugh laugh it was so funny. And Bernard laughed at me like he always had and I could have just climbed onto one of the padded chairs and sat upside down and slid all the way right off onto the floor and disappeared. I didn't even understand the joke, but it was on me. And there he stood thinking about my nappy and my shit and what an odd thing to bring up. I was confused and annoyed and all different things. And I thought why are they laughing? And it's not fair. And all of the things I always used to think. All those things I've always thought. Ha ha ha Rachel cried. You were meant to be my friend. I was meant to be the best person you'd ever met and he has reduced me to this. Again. The joker. I so small again.

Rachel asked Bernard and me to dinner at her house the following Sunday, and I was looking forward to it. Oh how I had learnt to love the pain by then. The next Sunday came and so we all came to the house – Rachel, her tragically optimistic father, Bernard and I. The meal was lovely. A widower who could cook. A man who had to cook. Chicken and mushrooms in a white wine sauce, with rice and greens – I remember the taste. A dish I would favour from then onwards. Pat did not come. Maybe she couldn't bear to see my face. How could you? We talked a lot about music, my way of impressing Bernard. I talked about eighties music and it made him very happy.

It made him impressed. It was as if that was all I had ever wanted. To be impressive, to impress. To make an impression on someone. On a man. On Dad. Would you be impressed Dad?

We ate the dinner and maybe it was just normal. I thought it was nice. Maybe he was just normal. Maybe nothing had ever happened. Maybe nothing has ever happened. He always was a joker. Oh, grow up. Won't you.

DADDO

You are gone but still so here. The worst of both worlds
You are gone and that is what has made you great
Gone and what has made me gone
No love of my own and looking for any other dad. It's hard to not
know things and to act them out anyway.
Harder still to know things and continue to act.
Little needer.
Little lost.
How do I stop?

JAMES

It's funny, because I spoke to my brother tonight and it's different. He's different now. We are adults. It may have taken him a while to get there but he's there. And he remembers all these things that I don't. But as soon as he said them I kind of did. He said that I made him laugh like no one else could. I cracked him up. He said that when we were kids and we were at Auntie Bet's and we had to amuse ourselves, we would do these games, we would do characters for each other to entertain ourselves. And I would be this old dog, Puff. This dog called Puff, who I now think was kind of an imitation of old Auntie Bet but we probably never saw it that way then. He said I'd put on this old man voice to be this dog, Puff, and he'd cry with laughter, and you know when he says it I almost remember. And he said that he sees now how naive he was and how horrible he was to me and I can see it in his face how bad he feels. And I tell him that it's okay. We were just kids. But you know it helps me. It touches me that he is telling me how bad he still feels about it. And it doesn't even seem that bad in my head, it just seems normal for kids. And I just have so much love and care for him now and I can see that he does for me too. And it's crazy how life is. It's crazy how we all have to survive when life is so strange and difficult and everyone is going through these things and no one else knows. And maybe it would be easier if we all just talked about it, you know. I ask him if he remembers anything about Bernard and Pat and he tells me that he thinks he's just blocked it all out and that makes me scared and it makes me sad and poor James. Poor James even though he's so big now. Poor James. No man to show him how to be a man. But he's doing okay. He's doing much better than the guys who treat me like shit. Big brother much better than the men who treat his little sister like shit. And he feels so much, too, like me. It is touching. I couldn't have guessed that I'd feel this way. He says that he doesn't remember anything at all from being a kid and that he doesn't understand when people say that they do. I say I think that neither of us remember anything before Dad died and he says maybe you're right. And he was older than me. I thought that it was just me! Maybe they're all lying. He says that he had a good time tonight. But of course he did. Because he had his girl there that he loves. I had no one. I walked home alone.

I look at my brother and I feel sad. He has done nothing with his life and I am successful but he has his girl and he is happy and I walk alone. I walk home alone and I have never felt so sad in my life and so empty. My brother loves her so much and takes care of her, and though he shouts for me to get home safe, there is no one there to make sure that I do. No man to care about me.

CAR

This time, Bernard locked me in the car on purpose, not forgot. He said that I had to go in the car because I was a naughty girl. I think maybe I got things wrong all the time. But I didn't do anything. I think that is why he was mad because he kept saying just do it, just do it you stupid little. He said he'd tell Mum if I didn't do it but I didn't want to. And then he said I had to go in the car. He said that Mum already knew and that naughty girls who don't do as they are told have to go in the car. It was dark but it was nicer than inside with Bernard. His skin looked like my fingers when I have a bath. He usually said that he forgot but he didn't that time.

BERNARD

Bernard is a truly good and kind man. He has dedicated his life to helping others and to the work of God. I have seen many pictures of him smiling and laughing, caring and hugging and kissing. I don't know God but I know that he is thought of in the same regard. They are holy men.

Bernard gives people food and clothes and shelter. He talks and laughs and sings. He wears funny coloured glasses, colours like purple or green or red. I think that this shows his carefree spirit and his warm attitude towards life. He runs a charity with a clever religious pun for a name, and that really just represents the kind of guy that he is. He is laid back and he never shouts. His only purpose in life is to offer a helping hand to those less fortunate. It really is an admirable life to lead. He is an unsung hero, you could say. He could be dead now, but I am sure that it would have been in the paper if he was. He is an inspiring and dedicated man.

BABY

Grow up, Baby. Grow up, grow up, won't you?

Oh what cruel fate it is to walk around in this adult body in this adult world but feel and live as a child. Why is it and why must it have happened to me, what am I meant to do now? How can I be expected to be this grown up thing and understand and cope when I am Baby?

And soon, soon you will take Mother too. Leave me out in the rain. What will Baby do then?

Thought I felt old when I was young but I am forever baby. I was old then, and I am young now.

ASSOCIATE

Now I sleep with other women's husbands.

HEART

Can't you sleep little bear?

I am a bastard by proxy and perhaps I should hang. Dad is still dead and I am still waiting for everything to be okay. But I'm not a bear, I'm a lion. I am your little lionheart, Dad.

I've forgotten the way that you spoke, Dad. The sound of your voice. I don't know that I ever remembered. There is this old home movie and in it you are talking to me. You dance with me and smile and say things into my little ears. But I cannot hear you, Dad. Your recorded voice seems a stranger's. I remember it differently, some made up voice in my head. But I was different then, too. I look at the video and I cannot relate to any of it. Cannot see myself in that poor little thing. Cannot see anything in you, Dad, though you are everything.

In part of the video, we are at little Catherine's christening. It is Christmas time and John Lennon and Yoko Ono are singing

'War is Over'. The camera bumps awkwardly across the room, a pub which is still there but has lost its charm, across ciggies and pints, glasses of wine, suits, smoke. And then we zoom to good old Dad holding little Catherine who is in a little white dress. My head in line with his though he is so much bigger, his big face pressed against mine, tiny. He sways around holding his baby. Singing those soft John words into my tiny ears. I'd do anything to hear it now.

Little Catherine, in her heart of hearts

I love Daddy the most.

Sitting in your chair. I can see living room, and the black, velour, three-piece suite. The background is fuzzy, foggy, but those sofas are effulgent. I look at the armchair in the corner and it feels soft and sat in. It feels safe. It feels like a place before everything went wrong. I have seen this chair in photographs. I have sat in this chair but it has gone. The walls are pink and cigarette smoke curls up against them. It is heartbreaking. It is afternoon but the light is not harsh. I want to see my father in the chair but I can only see myself. A child sat in the chair; her whole body fits on the seat. She is three, or four. I look into my eyes and I cannot see anything. No signs of what is to come. Her hands rest on the seat. She too looks as though she is waiting for something. She waits, a child forever. She looks as though she could speak

I look down into a box of records that feel like they are my own. It is dark, the kind of dark in a bar. Lights are twinkling and I see lots of familiar faces, I think. Everyone's backs are turned to me. I see the backs of people's heads and I think that I must know them. I pick out a record that I know my father will like and I rest it on the side ready to play. I look out for him

You smelled like cigarettes and I loved that smell before I even knew what it was. I would sit with you in your chair while you drank tea and smoked ciggies. Sit on you. Stand on your legs. Everything is so big when you are small! And Dad was big. You used to blow the smoke from your mouth and it would spill out, meandering wonderfully up, up, up. You'd do shapes just for me. Circles, and hearts, and stars. Magic.

From the memories that I think I have, it is hard now to tell which are my own. Perhaps none. My head has been filled with stories of you. Naive additions and mutations litter a child's recollections. That time you brought me a bottle of orange Lucozade home after work. I lay on my back on the carpet that is no longer there. And I inhaled the fizz and spluttered it back up again. I coughed the stuff out of the wrong hole and my eyes watered and you laughed. You picked me up and you made me safe again. But I don't know if that really happened.

Little Catherine, in her heart of hearts. I love Dad the most. If only I could have said how much, oh, would I have been able to avoid this dreadful end instead? Never got to say. There are those with fathers still alive that refuse them, that abuse them and hate them. But I with the best love and no one to give it to. All the chairs in the world won't change that.

Mum said you were asleep but you were dead.

LYN

But no, the cancer came for you instead, didn't it Lyn? I can only think about my mother and cry. She looks up and sees the two of you hand in hand. Sees the others gather around as well, I bet. Feels better and feels worse, too.

WASHED

I turn and I turn and I try to look in a direction where I cannot see your face. You will die soon, or perhaps you are already dead. It doesn't much matter any more.

You are blind to the fact that I am good. You are unkind, not I. Never, never, never, never, never.

Wash my eyes and I will see one day one day I will roar.

I wonder if you will go to heaven, Bernard? God loves you, and you love him. Or at least that's what you used to say. Have you changed your tune, I wonder. That gold fish meant you and Pat – but, doesn't it mean Christian? Good Christian. Good Samaritan. Are you good, Bernard?

I wonder, do you think about me and how does that make you feel? Do you talk to God about little Catherine? When I think of you, I still long for your approval and your love after all that's been done, for the love and approval of all those I hate. As though I exist somewhere lower even than hell.

I have always been drawn to religion. I like the way it looks and the way it sounds, though it is meaningless. My father was a religious man. Bernard, you take my father's faith, baseless though it must have been, and you piss on it. You are a sacrilegious sack of shit. What about Chloe, and what about little Heather? What about Catherine, huh? Maybe I just need somebody to blame. Need a big bad wolf. Need a villain to pin with this tragedy.

Heresy! Heresy! Heresay.

Talk to God and see if he wants you then.

DAYS

Some days I wake up and things feel different and I think is this what it's meant to be like all the time? It makes me happy that I can achieve it. Caravaggio says that some days are good and some are bad. As I stand looking up at the sky, people must think that it is my first time here and for a moment I don't even care. And one day, I'm sure of it, everything will make sense.

FOR

I suppose that these are the horses from which we are thrown.
We see things as we are, not as they are.
How do we best see? With eyes old or new?
How well do we rise after falling?

VINCERO!